# Wicked Baby

Tara Hanks

*Wicked Baby* by Tara Hanks

First published by www.pabd.com in 2004

This edition published by Allegra Press

Copyright 2016 by Tara Hanks

All rights reserved. Except for the use in any review, the reproduction or utilization of this work in whole or in part in any form by any electronic, mechanical or other means is forbidden without the express permission of the author.

While it is based on a true story this novel is a work of fiction and the events in it exist only in its pages and in the imagination of the author.

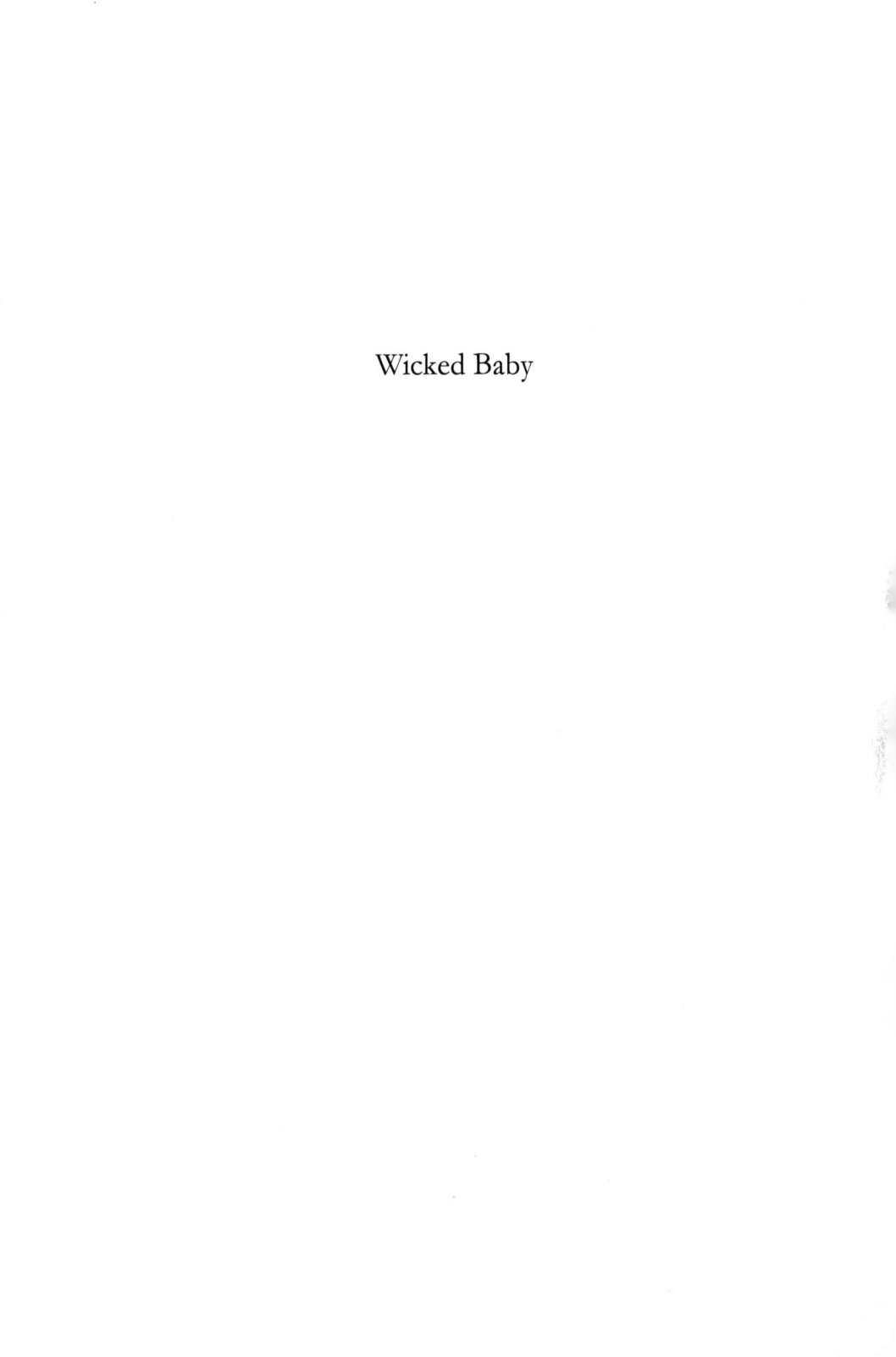

Wicked Baby

*To Andy, With Love*

*What we are seeing is the diseased excrescence, a corrupted and poisoned appendix, of a small and unrepresentative section of society that makes no contribution to what Britain is, still less what Britain can be.* — Harold Wilson, 1963

*Unto the pure, all things are pure.* — Titus 1:15

# PROLOGUE
## 1959

*My name is Christine. I live in Wraysbury, a village near Staines. I was born in a caravan, made from a railway carriage by my father. It was the only caravan in a village of bungalows.*

*Wraysbury was a dreary hole the rain had got into. Other girls were jealous of me right from the start. They came from the town. They hid in bushes and shouted insults as I walked downhill to school.*

*Even as a child I preferred the company of boys. I spent afternoons climbing trees and playing chess. Out in the woods where we lived, there were only boys.*

*Dad left early. Mum found another man, and he became my stepdad. The caravan grew, and our family with it. We were joined by half-brothers, aunts barely out of school, grandparents and pets. I never thought too much about anything. I looked out of the window and listened to the church bells ringing.*

*I was clever at first. I liked arithmetic, but loathed algebra. It was too slow and tricky for me. My stepdad taught me to drive and shoot, and I ran faster than any girl in my year. There was talk of putting me in races against other schools. But mum told me girls don't compete. I lost interest in school after that.*

*We never missed a thing, so close together. Not a clip round the ear or a hurtful remark missed its target. Knowing about each other didn't help us to understand one another. But we were in it together.*

~

*Mum had me too young. She'd throw tantrums when I got in the way. In her cups, she'd spill family secrets. This riled my stepdad, and they'd fight. He wouldn't marry her, and sometimes she'd leave. They were jealous, and didn't trust anyone.*

Rumours would fly about the husbands and wives they cheated with. That's how I earned my bad reputation, long before I knew what it meant to be bad. Playing with boys in the gravel pits, or stripping off to plunge in the river that ran behind the Thames.

I started a paper round on a bike with no brakes. Riding home one night, a man stopped me in an alley. He squeezed my arm and breathed in my ear. His breath stank of homebrew.

'I've been watching you, Christine.' I wondered how he knew my name. Perhaps he drank with my stepdad, on Saturdays in the Lion's Den. His leer reminded me of other men I didn't like to be alone with.

If my stepdad went near me, I'd give him a shove. Once, when I was sick, he smeared Vicks Vapo-Rub on my chest. Mum was in hospital, and he'd had a few drinks. Now I was old enough, he said, we'd go to Blackpool and live as man and wife.

After I made tea, he fell asleep. I sneaked a carving knife out of the drawer and kept it under my pillow. He never noticed it was gone. I washed up quietly, feeling hungover although I'd never been drunk. I didn't sleep a wink that night.

~

In the changing rooms at school, after games, boys stared at my tits. Boys held no mystery, and tits got in the way. It was older men who made the rules, men who held the key to life. I envied the freedom they had. The men I grew up with were shell-shocked from the war. I was underage, and they were just beyond my grasp.

But their mystery was also mine.

I left school as soon as it was legal. Mum signed me up to an employment agency. I worked in a factory, stencilling pictures of glamour girls onto ties; and in an office, taking dictation. I liked being out in the world. Most of all I liked the long, lingering looks men gave me. The attention made me happy, more acceptable to myself. I was photographed in a bikini and appeared in the Christmas issue of Titbits.

I started going out at night, and as my stepdad locked the caravan by ten, I came back less and less. I went to a pub called the Angel, where GIs came to drink. The American soldiers liked me. I drove in a limousine to parties at Langley airbase. I lost my virginity in the backroom of a bookshop in Staines. I survived unscathed, and was sorely disappointed.

Next time it was better. I stayed all night with a GI named Jim. He was hard-faced but sad (his wife didn't understand him). I smoked my first joint, and rested in my lover's strong arms. I soon woke up. The Yankees went home, and I realised that Jim had left me pregnant.

~

Sixteen, and I wished I were far away. If only I could escape. Life was different then. I couldn't withstand the shame of a bastard. My family would disown me and I would be ruined. I couldn't support a child. My child would live in an orphanage, watched over by nuns. I wished it dead.

I tried everything. Castor oil, gin and whiskey, until I blacked out or threw up. I hid in the woods or by the stream, confiding in no one. But it just grew bigger and kicked, a bump for people to talk about.

*I had to get rid of it, but I wanted it too. I pushed in a knitting needle, fumbling inside until my waters broke. I wept quietly, without hope.*

*The baby moved. It started pushing. Nine months, the nurse said. But only six months had passed. 'Nine months, just give me nine months. I'm not ready for this yet.'*

*Nobody heard. I couldn't cry; someone might hear me. Dull, heavy backache turned into a sharp, searing pain that came and went. The afternoon sun gave way to storms, beating down on our roof.*

*'Mum!' I cried.*

*An angry baby's howl drowned out my screams. He was hunched up and soaked in my blood. I grabbed hold of him as he reached out, fighting for air.*

*Mum ran in, shrieking, 'What have you done? Why didn't you tell me?' She got on the bike with no brakes and fetched the doctor. He took me away and put me to bed.*

*My son died in hospital. I named him James Peter Keeler. And still I didn't sleep.*

# CHAPTER 1
# 1960

It was a cold night in Hampstead, and Stephen had smoked his last Strand. He sat alone in the Nell Gwynn tavern, sipping Bloody Marys at six. By nine he was cursing his damned rotten luck. Supper was to be a blind date, a long-haired actress named Suzy Chang. She had missed her cue.

The bar door swung shut as he turned left of the high street. He tightened his scarf, avoiding shop-fronts and black ice. He dodged a ring of beggars on the Heath, plucking 'Mood Indigo' out of battered violins. They jeered, and his wallet stayed closed. He asked an old man for directions, then hurried on towards Japonica Gardens, to a private party.

The garden was neatly pruned, buttercups sprinkled in a late frost. A spare rib of a woman, starkers but for the bags under her eyes, answered the doorbell. Lovers in the raw blocked the narrow hallway, while Bing Crosby crooned from a Dansette. Stephen entered the house, catching a whiff of cheap wine and sex.

The invite had suggested nothing more taxing than a convention of bank clerks, and stayed unreplied. But it was Thursday night, and he was lonely.

'I'm starving,' he thought, his stomach growling. 'I wonder if there's a buffet — a glass of sherry will do.'

'Penny for your thoughts?'

'Not worth it.'

Victor sidled over, and lolled against the wall. A dog collar hung around his neck, and beads of sweat trickled down his chest.

'Whatever have you brought me to?' Stephen joked, ogling a few forlorn meringues abandoned on the sideboard. Whips and leather straps were laid out on a low table. 'All I wanted was a bite to eat.'

'Come to Mariella's this bank holiday.' Victor elbowed him. 'I'll show you something even you won't believe.'

They were occasional drinking partners at the gentlemen's clubs that spread like fever from Threadneedle Street. Victor invariably won at bridge.

He had first come to Stephen's surgery after a stag night, sporting a slipped disc.

'That's Mariella,' Victor said. A tall blonde removed her mink stole and sat on a comfortless chair. 'She married Hod Dibben last June.'

'I was a virgin bride. I'm not a virgin anymore.'

'And you are from ...?' Stephen asked.

'Czechoslovakia. Prague.' She yawned, and gazed down the corridor.

Stephen found Hod Dibben in the kitchen, a chicken drumstick lodged in his cheek. He owned the Black Sheep Club in Mayfair; Stephen had known him for years.

'How is our friend, Lord Astor?' Hod enquired jovially. 'I do so admire an aristocrat who mixes with the people. They are the rarest kind.'

Mariella tiptoed in, snaking her arms round her husband's neck. She wore a large diamond ring. Hod wore a rusty St Christopher's chain.

Stephen checked his watch. He had missed the last tube. Not wishing to fork out for a taxi, he decided to cadge a lift later on. Mariella smiled at him while Hod Dibben looked on; for now he was staying. His mind began to wander, not into desire, but the fear of solitude that haunted him each night. As the guests dispersed, the room was dark and silent. Beside him lay Mariella, naked and remote down to her red stilettos.

# CHAPTER 2

She got up and left the hospital. In the village, her name was mud. She took a job in London, as a waitress in a Greek restaurant on Tottenham Court Road. Her boss was fat as she was thin; he took pity on Christine and put her up, fed her. The hours dragged by for her, peeling, chopping and chastely smoking.

A young woman came to the restaurant one night.

'Why don't you come and work at the Cabaret Club?' she said, smiling warmly at Christine. 'That's where I work. The money's better and it would be much more fun. Mr Murray's always looking for new talent, and you're just the kind of girl we need.'

Christine raised an eyebrow. 'Me?'

The woman grinned and produced two cigarettes from a silver case. She placed one in the girl's mouth and the other in her own, sparking them both from a gold engraved Zippo.

'But what must I do?'

The woman sighed. Christine drew hard on her cigarette.

'Dance on stage. Listen to the music, feel the rhythm, and dance. I'll arrange an audition for you.'

'I'll think it over,' said Christine.

~

After a routine night's work at the club, Christine was introduced to Stephen Ward; by a fat, cigar-smoking property developer, a mutual friend. She danced with him, and then left for a late supper with her Persian boyfriend, who was studying Law at King's. She soon forgot the older man who paid for the evening's first brandy.

Slipping back to her mum's that weekend, she was surprised to find Stephen already there. His car was parked on the hill. He set the table for Sunday lunch. Poached, roast rabbit, and a creamy jam sponge from Fortnum and Mason's.

'However did you find me here?'

'I cadged your address from one of your boyfriends.'

'Who gave you mum's address?'

'Michael Lambton.'

'Oh!' She blushed. Lamb was a city gent who came to the club. He was a soft touch, bailing her out whenever she was broke. She had no idea how Stephen knew him.

Stephen drove her to his own Spring Cottage, at Cliveden where Lord Astor lived. The cupboards were packed fit to bursting, but the drawing room was threadbare as the first guest at a party. He poured her a tumbler of gin, and told her a little of his life story. Mostly he told her about the famous people he knew.

~

They met again on Wednesday at three; he picked her up from the boarding house where she was lodging. She studied her reflection in the rear-view mirror, while he filled her in with some royal gossip. She stifled a yawn.

Afternoon tea on the wrong side of Kensington; scanty gingham and nets framed a café's grimy windows. A woman stood outside at a bus stop, frowning, her bottle blonde bouffant flattened by rain. Stephen winked at her and she flashed him a brassy smile. When the sun had dried out he took Christine to St. James' park. They sat on a wrought iron bench, its black paint rusty.

'How long have you been working at that dreadful club?' he began.

'A couple of months, maybe. I don't remember. Anyway, it's not so bad.'

'I hope you're not going back there tonight. You must improve yourself, get in with one of the film studios. I know someone who could help you.'

'I don't want to improve myself, not yet.' Christine scoffed. 'I want to have fun, and enjoy life, like you do.'

Stephen chuckled. 'I like you very much, Christine, more than any girl in a long time. It's nearly five o'clock. Let's go and put our feet up at my place.'

An orange sofa and a round, glass-topped table were the only signs of life at 13, Wimpole Mews. Stephen put the pot on to boil and reached for the coffee jar.

'Get the cups out Christine, there's a dear.' The cupboards were otherwise empty. 'Coffee is frightfully good for the brain; why, I must drink twenty cups a day.'

He wrenched a packet of cigarettes from his pocket and quickly slipped one into his mouth. 'You're not a smoker, I hope?' he asked, without offering.

The flat was clean and functional as Christine wished for herself. With two bedrooms, a kitchen, living room and bathroom, it was small and economically furnished.

'This is such a lovely little flat, and so neat.'

She crept into the bathroom, locked herself in and ran clear, hot water through the tap. She bent over the porcelain tub and listened to the steady flow. Hot water fascinated her. There had been a bathroom in the caravan where she grew up, but no running water. Nine other tenants shared the bathroom at her lodgings. It was filthy.

She brewed coffee in the kitchen, and brought it into the living room where Stephen was sitting on the orange sofa. She set the tray on the glass table and poured milk into the coffee. 'How many sugars?'

'Two baby, always two. I wish you'd come and live here. I feel that I've known you all my life.'

She watched him over the rim of her cup, wondering if he was a dirty old man. 'Are you married?' she asked. 'I'm not very sexy, you know.'

'I don't want to make love to you, silly. I just like your company. I was married once and I certainly won't make that mistake again. I'm at the surgery most days and you're out in the evenings. It could work very well.'

## CHAPTER 3

At ten o'clock in the morning, chairs were stacked and tables cleared for polishing, as Mandy arrived for her audition. The club was a shabby let-down, the painted walls soiled and flaky. Faded red lamps had gone limp, as if startled.

But the job was hers, and Mr Murray wished there could be more girls like Mandy; skinny, flat chested, polite. 'You must start tonight, my dear. Have you found digs yet? I may be of help.'

A pretty, red-haired girl strode across the stage, scowling as he introduced Mandy. 'I've been here for ages,' she spat. 'We don't stand on ceremony for new girls.'

Mr Murray beamed, and clasped Mandy's hand. 'That was Miss Keeler,' he beamed. 'She's rather flighty these days. Pay no attention to Christine, Miss Rice-Davies. You have nothing to worry about.'

~

'Know your enemy ... better the devil you know.'

Christine was fond of proverbs; like cigarettes, they gave her reasons to go on. She had not kept Mandy at arm's length, as she'd hoped. They went to the same parties and fancied the same Arab boys.

Mandy was delicate and cunning as a cat. Christine was older and wiser, and looked down her nose at Mandy Rice-Davies. But the girl was persistent, and besides, she had her uses.

They walked out on Percy Murray and scraped a living as models, going to castings every day. Mandy never stopped fretting over where the next paycheque was coming from, but Christine wasn't fazed by uncertainty.

'What you need is a boyfriend,' she told Mandy. 'An older man, someone with real money.'

Mandy inherited other girls' lovers like a sister's hand-me-downs. She met Christine's most recent ex, Peter Rachman, over lunch at the Savoy. They gulped down cream pastries at the Polish Daquise, and he drove her to Pall Mall.

He was short, fat and bald. A Polish immigrant, his belly stretched wide by malnutrition. He used a sun lamp, and preserved his tan with expensive lotions; he wore silk shirts, cashmere suits and crocodile shoes.

'He's in property, raking it in,' said Christine.

Sex, for Peter, was a daily routine, like drinking a glass of water or brushing his teeth. Every afternoon, Mandy waited in her Bryanston Mews maisonette, owned by him. The curtains were drawn while she listened to Nat King Cole and read a chapter from *Forever Amber*.

She recognised his footsteps; he was her only visitor at this time of day. As he opened the door she was already undressing.

~

Like Christine before her, Mandy asked few questions, but allowed his secrets to slowly unravel. Peter rarely indulged in absolute truths. He worked in the East End, where all the young gangsters were making deals.

'England lets everyone in, even blacks. But it doesn't give them a home. That's what I do.'

They drove through a web of terraced streets, blacked-out windows wound cautiously down. But they never went inside the flats.

'Simple, those blacks — ten to a room, won't be parted. Don't know how to use a toilet. Primitive.' He sneezed into his monogrammed handkerchief, and opened the glove compartment. Inside was a gun.

'A man of my stature has dangerous enemies. Don't think twice about using it.'

They drove on to a casino, or Raymond's Revue Bar.

Light relief came in the form of Christine; Mandy looked forward to her dropping in. They would lie together in the king-size bed, sharing cake and reading comics like the schoolgirls they had been.

Suddenly Christine was an expert on Peter. 'He chases people with dogs and guns. How can you live with that on your conscience?'

In conversation with Peter, Christine was a forbidden subject. 'I don't want you mixing with that wicked girl — she'll land you in trouble.'

# CHAPTER 4

'I want you to cook tonight.'

Christine looked up from last month's *Tatler*.

'Why, who's coming — anyone I know?'

She loved to cook for Stephen, and did whenever she stayed at Spring Cottage. But although Wimpole Mews was their home, it had never been lived in. It was a meeting place for friends. She pestered him to replace the gas ring with a proper stove, but he wouldn't cough up.

'A gentleman is dropping by to discuss a business matter. You must dress to impress, little baby.'

'Well, I suppose I could rustle up a roast.'

Stephen was up to something, but he wasn't letting on. She left him to it.

In the queue at the butcher's, bundled among housewives and kids sent on errands, she remembered the cluttered caravan of her past life, ladling soup into bowls for her aunties and cousins.

Dinner was served by Christine, reined in by pan-stick and a heavy, beaded dress. She ate the leftovers in the kitchen.

'Delicious girl ... I mean, tasty meal.' Mr Hollis had been sent by MI5. He knew Stephen by hearsay.

'I have a favour to ask of you. I was recommended to you by my associate, a patient of yours.'

Stephen washed down a cut of lamb with red wine. It stuck in his throat.

'A Russian naval attaché arrives next week on state business. Eugene Ivanov. A most agreeable fellow, for a Russian.'

'That's marvellous! It's high time our countries put an end to this damned cold war.'

'I am not here to talk politics.' Mr Hollis downed his drink in one mouthful. 'Doctor Ward, you are an artist, a man of the world ... a cultured man, who could keep a lonely Russian amused. I don't have time to socialise, but we at the Service would be grateful if you did us the honour of meeting our captain. Ambassadors are only human — they need steering in murky waters.'

'Can I top you up?' Stephen twirled his glass by the stem. Mr Hollis indicated a small measure. 'It is perfectly safe, isn't it? I would tell you immediately if Comrade Ivanov planned to defect.'

'Or if he made any propositions to you regarding British intelligence.'

'But of course!' The idea of espionage excited Stephen. 'I could inform you of any Russian secrets he cares to disclose.'

'Should he be so rash. Ivanov is no fool, I assure you.' Mr Hollis consulted his watch. 'I can arrange an interview. It has been a profitable evening. Now perhaps you could ask your girl to call me a cab?'

# CHAPTER 5
# 1961

The lights came up one by one as the final credits rolled. Christine, sitting in the back row, withdrew her knee from Major Jim Eynon's tight grasp, and stood up for the national anthem.

'Wasn't it magnificent?' he said, as they walked arm-in-arm into the daylight. She felt warm and protected in the beaver jacket he had bought her.

'Oh, the film ... yes, it was great.' She had seen it before, but she didn't want to spoil it for him. He was reliable and kind. Every three months, when he was on leave, he took her to Leicester Square. It was always some dull, ponderous war film, and always an hour too long.

He hailed a cab. She had been hoping to go for dinner somewhere posh, but followed him in anyway.

'I'm attending a gala this evening, Christine. Can we go back to your flat for a while?'

She instructed the driver, and checked her gold watch discreetly. They still had a couple of hours before Stephen got back from the surgery. She didn't want him to know about the Major; she was sure he'd interfere.

Back in her days at Murray's, the Major had been her biggest fan. He was fifty-three, a little older than Stephen, but the resemblance ended there; he was quiet and reserved, a colonial type based in Peru. She led him into the flat, and then to the bedroom. He sat on the bed and unbuttoned his fly, watching her undress.

'This won't take long,' she thought, kneeling at his feet.

'I'm glad to see you've settled somewhere, my dear.'

He left twenty pounds on her bedside chair, picked up his coat and hat, and hurried downstairs to the taxi that waited. As it drove off, she stripped the bed and gathered the sheets, starting up the twin-tub in the kitchen.

When Stephen came in at seven, she was reading her horoscope in *Woman's Realm*.

'Hello, little baby! What does the future hold — will you pay your share of the phone bill?'

'Oh, very funny, Stephen. I had a call from the agency today — remember the casting I went to last week? Well, they're taking me to Paris to model next year's teenage fashions! Imagine that? I've never been abroad.'

'But that's super, Christine! Didn't I say you could do better than dancing in that grotty club? But how are you going to manage until then?'

'I'll cope — don't I always?'

'I must introduce you to a friend of mine. Have you met Charles?'

'Charles who? I don't think so.'

'He's a very rich man, and I happen to know he loves brunettes. He'll keep the wolf from the door — no strings attached. Why don't I ring him now and set up a date for tonight?'

'I can't be bothered, Stephen, but maybe another time.'

She took the magazine into her bedroom and lay on the bed while a bath ran. She fingered the notes that the major had given her, thinking, 'I can't tell anyone else about this.'

## CHAPTER 6

Driving out of London, the clubs that stank of beer and sweat. London in July was hot and heavy as a rush-hour ride on the tube. They swept past the airport, on the road to Maidenhead. Christine's hairdo tangled in the breeze.

'A party in the country is just the ticket, little baby.'

Stephen pulled over at a bus stop where a young girl waited.

'Aren't you the baker's daughter? Hop in. We're off to Cliveden, don't you know. We'll sneak you in for a sherry, if you promise to behave yourself.'

~

Stephen stood on the balcony, above a wide stone terrace. Cliveden was set over four hundred acres of land. In a corner was Spring Cottage, and beside him was Lord Astor, who let out the cottage for one pound a year.

They'd met at the Dorset Square surgery when Bill was hurt in a hunting accident. After the hunt each Saturday, Stephen treated Bill's back. Bill had loaned Stephen a thousand pounds, with no pressure to repay.

The cottage was large enough to entertain girls. Parties began at the big house and continued at Stephen's, after Bill's wife Bronwen had gone to bed.

~

'Haven't you brought a bikini, Christine?'

'I was in a hurry. It's in the wash, at home.'

She picked a one-piece from a pile in a cupboard. She went to the poolside, eyes darting across the water.

The evening stars turned on and twinkled.

'This really is a magical place,' she thought, staring into the endless cloudless horizon. 'How do people get to live here? I'd never meet a soul in a house like this. I'd just wander, and bump into ghosts. '

She shivered. A strap slipped. She dipped her toes in the water. Stephen was on the other side.

'Take off the swimsuit,' he said. 'Go on, I dare you.'

A few bored guests sloped off as dusk became dark. Refreshments were served in the ballroom.

'Alright then, you win. I'll go for a swim while it's quiet.'

She dove in and swam. She'd paddled midstream as a child, while her mother hung washing on a line. None of Stephen's rich friends had time to swim; only at weekends, in country house like this.

The guests reappeared, drinking brandy and smoking cigars. She gazed at them; some of the women were actually wearing tiaras. The spotlight turned on her; she blinked.

Two men in dinner jackets laughed at her. One was Lord Astor. The other was tall, with a bald patch. He spoke to her.

'Christine, is that you? I'm Jack.'

'Jack Profumo,' said Bill. 'He's our Minister for War, Christine.'

She swam to the far end of the pool, grabbed a towel, and climbed out. Hearing Stephen, She covered herself.

'Now you're for it, little baby!'

All eyes were upon her. Her hair dripped. She ran to the house, past women in taffeta gowns.

~

Sunday came, hotter than Saturday night. The last guests returned to the pool. Christine bit the lemon in her glass, and lay on her front.

'I've never met a Russian,' she told Captain Ivanov, who sat beside her. 'Are you a communist — or a refugee?'

'I'm a diplomat, my dear. You must call me Eugene.' While she studied the man, Jack Profumo watched. He came closer and knelt between them.

'Fancy a race, Eugene?'

Jack and Eugene jumped in the pool, while Stephen and Christine stood by. She expected a narrow contest, but Jack won easily.

'I reckon you cheated,' she said as he climbed out, passing him a towel. 'I bet you were using your legs ... he's in much better shape than you.'

'My dear girl, of course I did. I would have lost otherwise!'

'That will teach her to trust the British,' Eugene whispered to Stephen.

# CHAPTER 7

'At night, I like to drink vodka.'

Eugene's voice was husky as the bourbon they had shared on the train back to London. Christine led him upstairs for a nightcap.

'You're so patriotic. You haven't stopped talking about Russia since you left.'

'Only a week ago, but already I miss the Soviet Union.'

'Isn't Russia cold? I hear it snows there in July.'

'Moscow is hotter than London tonight. Russia is vast, much bigger than Britain.' He grinned, flashing sharp, white teeth. 'We do not have your English smog and rain.'

'Stephen's always moaning about the weather. The damp gets to his bones. He's nearly fifty, he lies about his age.'

Eugene stretched and yawned. 'What a fine, warm day it has been! In Russia, good weather is enjoyed by all the people.'

Christine filled his glass to the brim, and paused for thought.

'Just imagine! A Russian man and an English girl, drinking together like friends.'

'Stranger things have happened, Christine.'

'And in Stephen's flat! What will he say when he gets home?' She giggled. Eugene removed his jacket.

'You shouldn't let him tell you how to behave.'

'Stephen's just a friend.' The vodka rushed to her head. She loosened his tie, unbuttoned his shirt; he had the hairiest chest she had ever seen. Making no effort to resist, he cleared his throat and spoke carefully.

'I have a wife, Maya, who lives with me in the Soviet Union. She is a schoolteacher. She's not as pretty as you, but I love her very much.'

She fingered his breeches, slid her hand inside. He grunted something in Russian.

'You can trust me,' she murmured. 'I can keep a secret.'

The key turned in the lock.

'Oh, shit! It's Stephen!'

He sprang to his feet, dressing hurriedly. She bolted into the kitchen while he straightened his tiepin.

'Anyone home?' Stephen punched on the time-light in the hall. 'Oh, I say. Are you staying the night, Eugene?

~

She stood in the kitchen, frying eggs in a pan.

'Are those for me? I could eat a horse.'

Stephen sat down at the table, unfolded Monday's *Times* and lit up a waking cigarette.

'You're very quiet, little baby.' She smiled faintly at him. 'My goodness, is that a blush?'

'The eggs are for Eugene.' She coughed.

'Well ... I'm afraid he's gone. I met him on the landing, dashing off somewhere.'

'He's a married man.' She sighed. 'What was I thinking of?'

Stephen tutted mildly, and gave her his cigarette. She went to the window, gazed out at the businessmen scuttling off to the city, like ants shrouded in an early mist. She tied her white towelling robe fast, shivering.

'You went to bed with him, didn't you?' Stephen grinned. 'You are a naughty baby. I never know what you'll get up to next.'

'So what if I did, Stephen?' she snapped. 'It's my life.' She flicked ash onto the formica table.

'It may not be for much longer.' He chuckled. 'I spoke to Jack Profumo last night. He's very keen on you. Don't you see? With Eugene on one hand, and Jack on the other, we've got a nice little set-up right here. In fact, we could start a war.' He flipped the eggs onto plates, and took a large bite. 'Eat them before they cool, Christine. We won't eat as well in Siberia.'

## CHAPTER 8

Jack sounded the horn, waiting outside in a red mini.
'Is this your car?'
Christine slammed the door and squeezed in beside him. Their knees knocked. This car was too small for a man like Jack Profumo.
He pecked her on the cheek. 'We have to be discreet,' he whispered hotly, exploring her ear with his tongue. An old woman at a crossing squinted and scowled.
'It's very cosy in here.' Christine hitched up her green linen skirt. Having driven twice round Regent's Park, they stopped in a siding. Jack grabbed her breast but she pushed him away.
Dishevelled, they walked in the sun. Christine's green bolero jacket covered her shoulders. Jack gripped her tiny waist.
'Where are we going?' she asked. 'There's a pub round the corner. I'm thirsty.'
He shook his head, gently smacking her backside. 'Let's lie down for a while.'
'Not here!' She looked down upon burnt stubs of grass. 'Anyone could see.'
'Don't worry,' he laughed. 'I live over there.'
A row of townhouses lay beyond the park gates. He led her to the door of a grand, silent house with dead fish-eyes for windows.
'It comes with the job,' he smiled.
She thought of her parents in Wraysbury. Her mother and stepdad worked as hard as this man, yet they had done without water or electricity for years.
They climbed the steps and Jack opened the door. In the hall were a stuffed tiger and a caged parrot. 'Hello Jack,' it squawked. 'Hello Valerie.'
To the left was a dining room with marble floor, cold as ice. His last dinner guest had been the Queen. Christine couldn't imagine taking tea with Elizabeth.

At the top of the staircase was Jack's office, holding a drinks cabinet and three telephones on a varnished bureau. 'The black one's a scrambler. I use it when I'm talking to the Prime Minister. It distorts our words so that nobody else can understand ... you never know who might be listening in.'

He guided her into the master bedroom. She sat on the four poster bed, folding her clothes in a neat pile. The striped sheets were spotless; she wondered who washed them. He undressed quickly.

He pressed his lips against hers, bit her mouth and it bled. He fell on her like a lead weight, and she sighed.

~

'Checkmate.'

Eugene swept the pieces off the chessboard with a wink. They spilled onto the carpet. He rose and reached for the mantelpiece, where a bottle of cognac stood.

'To world peace,' Stephen toasted. Eugene raised both eyebrows. He fumbled inside his navy blazer, found cigars for them both.

'Where is Christine tonight?' He breathed in deeply.

'She's out on a date — but she'll be sorry to miss you. She fancies you madly, you know.'

'The feeling is mutual — she's a lovely girl.' Eugene laughed through the smoke. 'Have I many rivals?'

Stephen smiled furtively. 'One or two — maybe more. Tonight she's with a new lover — Jack Profumo.'

Eugene spluttered. 'Jack Profumo — the Minister for War?' He was incredulous.

'Yes — but of course it won't last. Jack is a very busy man.' Stephen let his cigar rest in an ashtray. Eugene clenched his fist, punched the air.

'But really, this is marvellous news, don't you see? How well do you know Jack Profumo?'

'Oh — a little. I count him as a friend.'

'Has he ever talked with you about the situation in West Berlin? Everyone in Russia knows the allies are sending warheads there.' His eyes narrowed and focused on Stephen. 'Do you know when that might be?'

Stephen shrugged. 'I have no idea.' Eugene pulled his armchair nearer.

'Maybe you could find out for me. A word in Profumo's ear, my friend. Strictly confidential.'

'Look, I really don't think ...'

'I'm sorry, Stephen. I have put you in a compromising position. Perhaps I should ask Christine instead.'

'Are you sure?' Stephen asked. 'Christine is so young, a simple girl — not calculating. Would it be fair?'

Eugene ground out his cigar. 'My offer is open to you, friend. I could make it worth your while. I have many rich friends in Russia who would be glad of the information.' He bent down and tied his right shoelace. 'Now, I must be going. My friends at the embassy are waiting for me.'

## CHAPTER 9

Stephen awoke on the sofa, still in his dinner jacket. He had fallen asleep after Eugene left. He went to the bathroom and shaved. The mirror's image was stark and unforgiving; his eyes were red and his silvery hair stuck out in tufts. He put a pan of water on the boil. The telephone rang.

'Doctor Ward? Wagstaffe here.' (Keith Wagstaffe was Mr Hollis's colleague at MI5.) 'The ambassador took a shine to you, eh? His third visit this week, and it's only Wednesday.'

Stephen gazed at the chess pieces scattered across the living room. Cradling the receiver, he paced about, repeated what Eugene had said.

'That's a remarkable story,' said Wagstaffe, when he had finished. 'He has taken you into his confidence, Ward.'

'I was just about to contact you. I'm as shocked as you are.' Stephen poked his head out of the open window. The milkman waved up at him.

'Christine's the young lady who cooks so well?' Wagstaffe flicked through the catalogue of a model agency, and found a picture of her on a swing. Mr Hollis had told him all about her. 'Tell me, where did she spring from?'

'She's a dancer. She models. She has no family connections, no money of her own.'

The agent cleared his throat. 'But she is making connections — dangerous ones. Mr Profumo is unusually impulsive. Does he know Ivanov has designs on her?'

'He knows that Christine has other lovers.' An unlit cigarette dangled from Stephen's mouth. 'Jack and Eugene both met her at Cliveden some weeks ago.'

'I had hoped Ivanov might be persuaded to defect. An affair with a girl, a few choice photographs would settle the matter. But it seems our ambassador has different ideas. It is most inconvenient.'

Stephen thumbed a recent sketch of Christine. 'If she were to ask Jack about the missiles ...' he began, hatching a plan in his mind. With pretty girls at his disposal, he'd go far in the Service. But of course, he couldn't tell her about it.

'Then Eugene Ivanov might be useful to us yet,' the man from the service said. 'The girl can supply the bait, and neither should be any the wiser. I'll give it some thought, Ward, and we'll be in touch with Mr Profumo soon.'

The man rang off abruptly. Stephen made a dash for the kitchen, where the pan had boiled dry. He had breakfast alone in a café, near the surgery, and thought again about Eugene's offer. Perhaps he could persuade Christine to talk to Jack, find out something to keep Eugene happy.

Surely no real harm would be done; he might even bring England closer to Russia. He left his meal half-eaten and hurried to Dorset Square, greeting his secretary with a kiss on the cheek.

~

'A word in your ear, Jack.'

'What the devil — oh, it's you, Norman. What can I do for you?'

He sat down on a crumbling wall with Norman Brook, the cabinet secretary. The old man stooped forward, catching his breath. His grey eyes were fixed on a maple tree, its leaves curled dry.

'A long hot day?' he remarked, at leisure. 'Not a pleasant one for you.'

'No.' Jack's hands dug deep in his trouser pockets. 'I thought question time would never end, with Harold Wilson grilling us over what's to be done in Berlin.' He spotted his car in the distance. He was just a short drive away from a stiff drink and a lovely young girl. 'Don't those Labour MPs ever get tired of chasing communists?'

'Wilson wants to keep the Russians out as much as you or I. He's an opportunist, that's all.' Norman Brook's white quiff stood still in the breeze. 'Now Jack, this may surprise you, but we may share a mutual friend. Do you happen to know Stephen Ward, my osteopath?'

'Yes — he drew my wife's portrait not so long ago.'

'Jolly fellow, isn't he? He took me to a party a while ago, with that Russian who's in town. I forget his name. Always well dressed — rather suspect in a Soviet, don't you think?'

'You must mean Eugene Ivanov. I had no idea they were such good friends.'

'Oh yes. Ward's a gadfly — and a matchmaker. I expect Eugene's had every girl in Mayfair by now.' The cabinet secretary nodded to Jack, and coughed. 'You've met him before, I suppose?'

'Several times. He was at the Astors' ball with Ward.' Jack remembered their race in the pool.

'He's not entirely trustworthy, you know.' Norman Brook plucked a daisy from the grass below, prising the petals off one by one. 'Our sources believe he may be spying on Ward. And Ward's a dreadful chatterbox, you know.' (Brook had been tipped off that morning, by the editor of the *Telegraph*.) 'I never discuss anything beyond cricket with him, though he's harmless enough.'

Norman Brook raised himself with the aid of a stick, patting Jack on the shoulder. Jack followed him to the taxi rank where he hailed a cab to Belgravia. Jack waved goodbye, then walked back to his office at the House of Commons. He dialled Christine's number, but there was no reply. She would be waiting for him at the Dorchester Hotel, and if he hurried he might still catch her.

~

Stephen busied himself in the kitchen while Christine stood under the shower. He left the dishes to soak and returned to the living room. He sat on the edge of the sofa, reading yesterday's news.

On the front page were photographs of John F. Kennedy, the young American president; Harold Macmillan, Britain's dyed-in-the-wool Prime Minister; and Profumo.

"CRISIS AT BERLIN," the headline ran.

Christine emerged from the steam, threw on Stephen's dressing gown and wrapped her hair in a towel. She peeked in the mirror, but it was all steamed up. She joined Stephen and, after a sip of the coffee he'd made, switched on the hairdryer.

'Can't you turn that down a notch?' Stephen grumbled. 'Here, take a look at this.' He passed her the inky broadsheet.

'You know I never read that stuff.' She yelped her surprise. 'Oh, it's Jack! Doesn't he look solemn? At least the president's smiling.'

But Stephen wasn't listening. He read over and over the words of Harold Macmillan: "We cannot countenance interference with Allied rights in Berlin ... It is a principle that the peoples of the Western World will defend."

He bit his lip. 'Jack must be feeling the strain. There are troops to round up for Germany, and our boys stuck in Kuwait. No wonder he took a mistress, eh, baby?'

'Jack's very careful — and I'm not his mistress. I'm just a girl he sees now and then. He says I help him relax.'

'I'll bet, you wicked baby!' They both laughed, and after a moment he added, 'So tell me — what do you know about the bomb?'

'What bomb?'

'The one America's sending to West Germany. Surely he must have mentioned it to you.'

'I don't know about any bomb! We never talk about his work — or mine,' she shrugged.

'You could ask him next time,' Stephen replied. 'You could find out when the bomb's due, just for me.'

She floundered. 'As if Jack Profumo would tell me a thing like that!'

Stephen laughed. 'Don't be cross, old girl. I was only having you on.'

'Sometimes I wish I'd never met you, Stephen. I don't understand you at all.'

He picked up the telephone as she walked away.

## CHAPTER 10

Jack arrived the next day in his other car, a white Rolls Royce. Christine curled up on the padded leather seat. The car purred through the city. They drove past Downing Street and the barracks Jack governed.

'Have you ever wanted to live by yourself?' he asked.

'Sometimes I think about it, but never for long. It's cheaper to share, and I prefer the company.'

'But what can you and Stephen have to talk about?' Jack raised an eyebrow. 'He's so much older than you, and such an odd fish.'

'I like older men — if they're young at heart. You're not jealous of Stephen, are you?'

'It's foolish, but I am.' An eager smile lit up his face as he drove across Tower Bridge. 'If you had your own flat, somewhere near Parliament, I could visit every day. You could meet my friends. Just think, darling, wouldn't it be grand to live on the river?'

She held up a compact mirror and dabbed at her face with a tissue. 'Honestly, I'm happy as I am.'

He was quiet as they drove home, kissing her as they turned into Wimpole Mews. He parked on the kerb and let down the seats.

'Where are you from, Christine?' He ran his fingers through her hair.

'Wraysbury. It's in Berkshire — you wouldn't know it. My parents aren't well off.' She blushed.

'That's what I suspected.' He took out his wallet and placed a crisp twenty-pound note on her lap. 'Here's something for your mother.'

'I don't want your money. Besides, my mother wouldn't approve.'

He shook his head, puzzled. 'Well, go to the hairdresser, or the manicurist or wherever you girls go nowadays.' He left the note on the seat, kissing her forehead. 'I'll ring you after the weekend, and we'll go out for dinner. Only keep it private, darling. I'd rather not bump into Stephen if that's alright with you.'

~

Mandy stood by the gate to London Zoo, wearing a salmon-pink twinset with pearls, pleated skirt and court shoes. She was five minutes early. Christine hopped out of a taxi.

'Can you lend me three shillings? I'm all out of change.'

Christine ran to the ticket office, waving a ten-pound note at the cashier while Mandy paid the driver. They strode in, cutting across the lawn to buy ice cream.

'Guess who I've been having an affair with?' Christine teased. 'Jack Profumo — he's the Minister for War, you know.'

'You have stepped up in the world.' Mandy peered at Christine. 'You must introduce us sometime.'

Christine thrust a blue envelope into Mandy's gloved hand. 'Too late, I'm afraid.' The letter came from him, peppered with excuses. ('Something's blown up and I can't make it ... won't be able to see you again until September ... take care of yourself and don't run away.')

'Do you think he's found another girlfriend?' Christine asked, her tone deliberately light.

'Oh, no.' Mandy pulled off her gloves. 'Maybe his wife found out. She's an actress, isn't she?' She had read about the Profumos in *Who's Who*.

They stopped near the birdcages. Two ostriches gawked at them. 'I've got one of those,' said Mandy. 'An ostrich feather hat. Peter gave it to me.'

They passed a group of bears, and stopped at the lions' cage. Christine went as close as she dared. A lioness, sheltering her cubs, growled. They sat on a bench by the mud-bath, and Christine lit up a cigarette.

'Do you think Stephen's a spy?' she asked. 'I mean, for the Russians?'

Mandy laughed. 'Not unless there's something in it for him.'

'He asked me to find out a secret — from Jack. It's about sending bombs to Germany.'

'I expect he was joking. Or maybe Eugene wanted to know.' It didn't add up. 'Did you tell Jack about this?' Mandy wriggled out of her cardigan as the sun burned down.

'God, no. I've never spoken to him about politics. I wouldn't know where to begin.'

'Is that why he dumped you?'

'Well, he wanted to buy me a flat, but I said no. Then he had to go away on business.'

'Don't you think it's strange? Perhaps he wanted to steal you away from Stephen. We all know Stephen's a dreadful gossip. He can't keep secrets for toffee — '

'— And Jack's a married man. Why didn't I see it before?'

They walked back to the entrance gate. Mandy's box-pleated skirt blew up in the breeze, earning a leer from an elderly porter. Then they were gone, lost to the underground. They jostled downstairs, hearing a distant rumble.

'I'd keep that letter if I were you.' Mandy handed it back. 'It might be worth money one day.' As the tube doors eased shut she jumped aboard, leaving Christine alone on an empty platform.

## CHAPTER 11

Stephen was among the first to arrive at the house on Hyde Park Square. He was greeted by Mariella, dressed in a black corset and cracking a whip. A naked, wrinkly man was strapped between two wooden pillars; his face was masked.

'Stephen.' Mariella passed him the whip with a smile. 'Give him the lash, and let Hermione have her turn.' She indicated the slight, powdered woman behind her.

He walked into the dining room and pulled up a chair, listening to the cries of the masked man as he was struck repeatedly.

Hod Dibben appeared at the foot of the stairs and sank onto a couch. His emphysema was clearly worsening, but he got by. 'Blast it, I've forgotten my inhaler,' he rasped. 'And the handcuffs.'

Stephen peeped through the gold velvet curtains out to the dark lamp-lit streets. He filched a cigar from an unclaimed case, grinning impishly. 'Do tell me, Hod — who is the masked man at the door?'

Hod yawned, exposing a mouthful of rotten teeth. 'I've been sworn to secrecy. He's a film director, from a distinguished family ... and he relishes his anonymity.'

The tables filled quickly and the squeals of the masked man were drowned out by low chatter. Mariella was the last to enter. She closed the door, kicking him onto the carpet.

'That's where you belong.' The man crawled under the table and whimpered. 'Shut up!' Mariella paced the room; the whip was in her hand. Hod lit the silver candelabra, and flames made shadows on the wall as a woman sniggered.

Dinner was served by young girls in frilly aprons and heavy mascara. Peacocks were served, cooked for the occasion, their heads and necks carefully skewered; bright tail feathers plucked from older birds added to the spectacle, with a side dish of badger.

A guest retched noisily. 'It's barbaric! And her' — she pointed to Mariella — 'she's a sadistic bitch!' Stephen recognised the woman, devoutly Catholic and a regular at these events. He went to her and began to massage her neck, while Mariella slipped a blindfold over her eyes, and Hod carved the peacocks with a long, thin knife.

'I'm getting awfully hot and bothered.' Stephen peeled off his shirt. Other men followed suit, while the women kept on their stockings and suspender belts.

~

Christine appeared much later; she spotted Stephen with a producer for the BBC, and hoped he was putting in a word for her.

Naked bodies surrounded her, people talked in low whispers and laughed loudly. Tired couples were sprawled on rugs. 'I'm the youngest person here,' she thought, 'but I've missed the party — it's all over.' Stephen's friend Mariella lay with three men on a waterbed, and a woman in silk underwear was playing on a piano.

Stephen strutted across in an untied robe and one rolled-down sock. 'Late again, little baby? You should have been here half an hour ago — some very serious people are letting their hair down tonight.' He pointed out a colleague from his surgery and a philosopher who guested on radio debates.

'It's a little quiet though, isn't it? I should have stayed at home — you know I don't like orgies. Who's that odd little man, and why has he got a mask on?' She followed the retreating figure with her eyes, as he carried a stack of plates into the kitchen.

'Now that would be telling.' Stephen smiled in a knowing, superior way that always irritated her. 'He's a dear friend of mine ... very high up in the Department of Transport.'

Mariella joined them, offering tangerines from a glass bowl. 'Look, Stephen!' said Christine. 'I haven't seen these since the war. I ate one once when I was a child — I won it at a church fete.' Mariella winked and Stephen chuckled. Christine peeled one, sucking each segment slowly.

An electric light flooded beneath the cloakroom door. Mariella, weary but curious, teetered in on six-inch heels. Her cupboard had been opened and dozens of shoes covered the floor. Among them lay her husband, sleeping, the spike of her blue stiletto pressed against his lips.

## CHAPTER 12
## 1962

It was just before midnight. Stephen stopped his car on Westbourne Park Road, took out his sketchpad and began to draw. A girl walked into the Lazy Days launderette, a satchel on her back. She wore a short dress slit at the thigh. In a year or two she might be tired and fat, a baby at her breast. He had caught her in her prime.

The girl waited among whirring machines until a large man in a zoot suit appeared. She gave him the bag, and he passed her a wad of banknotes.

'Let's get out of here,' said Christine.

They drove on through Paddington towards Notting Hill, braking for a woman who stood in the road.

'Looking for company, sir?' The woman smiled thinly. Her face was pockmarked, her skin pasty.

'Not tonight,' he replied. 'I'm with a friend.'

'What a pity.' She made for the street in her beaten-up slingbacks.

'Isn't she a fright?' Stephen giggled. 'An alcoholic or a dope fiend.' The woman slipped into an alley.

'Do you really think so?' Christine asked. 'What a nerve she's got! She must be forty-five.'

'Hmm ... wouldn't touch her with a bargepole. You'd make a killing out here. Perhaps I'll put you on the game.'

Christine laughed, despite herself.

'With your looks, and my brains...' His voice trailed off as police sirens wailed, and blue cars headed for Little Venice. A fight had broken out by the Grand Union Canal. An old man lay bleeding among piles of rubber tyres, his friends having scarpered ten minutes before.

They drove into Notting Hill Gate, where kids played barefoot on doorsteps, and the smell of rotting waste rose from the paving stones.

~

'Let's fill our bellies, baby.' They walked into the El Rio Café. Stephen ordered espresso, while Christine gazed at platefuls of rice and peas. A dozen black faces watched her, though nobody met her eye. The air was thick with smoke and the clock had stopped hours before.

'Somebody's got pot,' whispered Stephen, sniffing around. 'Do you think we could buy some here?'

'Maybe I'll go outside.' Christine got up while he settled the bill. The night air was cold. She approached a man.

'I'm looking for some, uh, weed.' His arm encircled her. Her head reached his shoulder and almost touched. He was bald and growing a beard. His red shirt was open.

'Oh.' The man tutted. 'You got ten shillings?' She paid him from her purse. Stephen was in the car, his hand resting on the steering wheel.

The man prodded her on the shoulder. He pressed a portion of grass, wrapped in tin foil, into the palm of her hand. She edged slowly off the wall. His breath warmed her neck.

'You come with me.'

~

She called for Stephen. The man led them down the street into a basement where boys danced shirtless in the dark to a scratched Charlie Parker record.

'What kind of music is this?' she asked.

'Be-Bop,' said Stephen. 'I don't care for it myself.'

The man, whose name was Lucky, passed Christine a joint.

'Thanks.' She inhaled, trying to follow the melody. Lazy bodies flopped to the floor, laughing, smoking and singing. Lucky moved closer as she lurched forward and vomited.

Stephen wiped her face with his handkerchief. 'Come along home,' he said, grabbed her arm, and dragged her to the car. Lucky watched them drive off, clutching the scrap of paper where Christine had written her telephone number.

## CHAPTER 13

She went back to the café where she'd met Lucky a week ago. He'd tried to reach her by telephone, but was fobbed off by that flaky doctor she lived with. He'd caught her in on Sunday and pressed her to meet him there again. His heart stopped when she walked in.

His leather jacket was zipped up to the neck, and a peaked cap cast a shadow over his face. He stood up, blocking her path. 'Let's go back to my place,' he said. 'I've got something for you.'

~

The front door was open. She fumbled for the light-switch, but the bulb was dead. They climbed four flights of stairs in darkness.

'I stole jewellery for you. I've got rings, an emerald, bracelets, chains ... diamonds, even.'

Christine gripped onto the bannister. The house smelt musty, like the boarding house where she'd lived before she met Stephen.

She sneezed as they reached the top. He kicked the attic door in. Dust and daylight dazzled them. He gripped her wrist and pushed her face down on the mattress.

'Let go ... where's the jewellery?' He climbed on top of her. 'Please don't hurt me ... I want to go home.'

'Shut up.' He breathed heavily. He pulled a knife from his pocket and let it touch her throat. 'If you don't let me fuck you, I'll kill you.' His dick was hard as he pressed it against her spine. She weakened. 'And don't even think about screaming. My brother lives downstairs and I've told him all about you. He knows what a loose bitch you are.'

She let him screw her, thinking, 'how stupid I've been. I knew I couldn't trust him. How on earth do I get out of here?'

~

They lay together in silence. It was night but she had no idea what time it was. He snored. She looked at him, head shaved, eyes closed. The room had a stale smell. She had to stop herself from puking.

The window was shut. It was narrow but maybe she could squeeze through. She would have to climb down somehow. She moved her foot off the bed to the floor, hoping to get to the door. He stirred, rolled on top of her and groaned, pushing her legs apart.

Morning came. He sat half-dressed on the bed, sharpening his knife with a stone. He brought a telephone from downstairs. The cable stretched just inside the door.

'You better call the doctor,' he mumbled, offering her the receiver. She took it eagerly and dialled Stephen at his surgery.

'Where did you go yesterday?' he asked. 'I had to cook for myself last night.'

'I'm at Lucky's.'

'I thought as much. Well, come home as soon as you can.'

Lucky cut her off.

'I have to go,' she said breathlessly. 'Stephen's mad at me.'

Lucky scowled. 'But you're my girl now! I want you to stay here.'

'I want it too ... but I have to keep him sweet, or he'll call the police on us.'

'I'll ring you in an hour then,' he said.

## CHAPTER 14

Lucky caught a bus from Bayswater to Wimpole Mews within the hour. Stephen stood up as the doorbell sounded.

'Please don't let him in,' Christine hissed.

Stephen tutted. 'Explain how you feel, and I'm sure he'll see sense.' He left her and answered the door.

'Where is she?' Lucky rushed upstairs. 'I want to speak to her alone.'

He was with another man whom Christine recognised from the El Rio Café. Lucky grabbed her arm and moved into her bedroom. The door banged. She screamed as he pinned her on the bed.

The man looked at Stephen, who shrugged. They went to the bedroom door.

'For God's sake, Lucky!' the man shouted. 'Get out of there.'

Lucky and Christine returned to the lounge. He touched her leg and she kicked him. He grabbed her by the throat and shook her. His friend prised him off her.

'Come on, let's go,' the man said. Lucky nodded, glaring at her.

They went.

'What are you going to do?' Christine asked.

Stephen frowned. Now her affair with Jack was over, she was sulky and unsettled. In fact, she was becoming a liability. If word got out that she was seeing a black man, his reputation would suffer.

'I'll call the police,' he said finally. 'That's what you want, isn't it?'

~

A fat, balding detective arrived, and accepted tea and biscuits with a grunt.

'What happened?'

'I've been attacked.'

'The girl's upset,' said Stephen. 'Why don't you have a lie-down, Christine? I can deal with this.' She hesitated for a moment, and then left them to it.

'I must be frank with you, sir.' Stephen sat on the edge of the sofa, boxing the detective in. 'I'm at my wits' end.'

'Has this happened before?'

'Several times. She's sleeping with a black man — a dope dealer, I think — and when they're not high, they fight.'

'It's not a solid case, then?'

'In my opinion, it's a waste of police time. I think we should let it stew.' He walked over to his glass cabinet and took out a bottle of brandy. 'Now, can I get you something stronger?'

# CHAPTER 15

'Darling, it's been too long ... where have you been hiding?' Paul Mann passed Christine an open bottle of champagne, and she drank freely. Paul was a friend of Stephen's.

She looked for Stephen but he was still at the bar, chatting up a waitress. Her first real night out since that time with Lucky; she'd been looking over her shoulder since then. (She'd got a bit of work, in an advertisement for Camay soap and as a contestant on a quiz show. At least she was making money.)

He still phoned her of course, late at night after Stephen had gone to bed. But it was three weeks since he had come to the flat — maybe he'd found another girl.

She made her way onto the dance-floor, feeling safe among friends. The All-Nighter was one of the new, late-license venues. Harry Belafonte was coming in the spring. Then she saw Lucky watching her from across the room. As he came closer, her face fell. She joined Paul in a huddle with two girls, with Lucky behind her. She whispered to Paul, and he turned round.

'We don't want any trouble,' Paul told Lucky.

He was dressed all in black, with a peaked cap like a soldier's. Chuckling softly, he shook his head and patted Paul on the shoulder, ignoring Christine.

'Let bygones be bygones,' he said. 'Want a drink?'

Several drinks later, a gang of them headed to Mandy's place. Stephen had gone home. They fought a lot now, and Christine preferred to stay away. Mandy was in America, and had asked her to water the plants. She slept there most nights. Maybe she wouldn't go back to Stephen, after all.

~

Christine smoked rapidly, stubbing the ends onto a saucer. She'd dispose of the evidence later. The room was filled with bodies, and noise. A girl named Pat had passed out behind the sofa, clutching an empty bottle of white wine. The light was switched off, and the smell of smoke was suffocating.

Climbing over discarded shoes, Christine plugged in Mandy's record player and sifted through a stack of LPs, settling on Johnny Mathis. She rolled a joint and lay back with it. How good life could be if Mandy never came back; perhaps she'd stay in the States this time, be a starlet or whatever she wanted.

She looked around the flat, wishing she had a place of her own. She knew as many rich, generous men as Mandy did; it was staying interested that was difficult.

~

She saw the axe smash through the wooden door. The door splintered.

'Lucky, stop. I'll let you in.' She turned the key, and they stood apart.

'How did you find me? Leave me alone.' The others grabbed their coats and ran — even Paul. Behind the sofa, Pat was gently snoring.

Lucky's face fell. He lifted the axe. 'I'll kill you this time ... get your clothes off.' She leaned against the wall. Lucky lunged forward.

He dragged into the darkened bedroom, threw her against its four walls and punched her face.

~

He rummaged through ashtrays, searching for cigarette butts. She felt cold and dirty. Two days or more had gone by, and nobody missed her. Lucky left the door open, so that Pat wouldn't run away. If Christine did what he asked, he wouldn't hurt her friend.

'You'll have to do it,' she whimpered. 'I can't go outside.' She stared miserably at her bruises. 'And get some eggs — I'll cook.' He went reluctantly, like a boy leaving home for his first day at school. She dialled 999 as he vanished into the street.

Christine hugged Pat, who was crying.

~

'You've done the right thing, Miss Keeler,' the officer said. It was the same man who Stephen had called to Wimpole Mews. 'Gordon's a nasty piece of work — we're charging him with Grievous Bodily Harm, on account of your injuries. You'll need to talk to a solicitor — I'm sure Dr Ward can find a good one for you.'

She walked out of the police station, trying to get her bearings. It was spitting rain. Two men approached her.

'I'm Lucky's brother, Jim,' said the first. He was large but timid, and stood with his hands in his pockets. 'He really loves you, he tells me all the time.'

'He raped me.' She tried to get away but the other man, lean and gruff like Lucky, stepped lightly on her toe.

'If this goes to trial, they'll crucify him. It'll break my mother's heart.'

She thought about going to court, and how worried her own mother would be, when all she wanted was to be free of Lucky.

'Drop the charges, miss,' the fat one pleaded. 'We'll make sure he stays away.'

She let go of her dead cigarette, and stamped it underfoot. 'Alright,' she sighed, 'I'll do it.'

~

'I want to drop the charges against Lucky Gordon,' she informed the officer on duty.

'Is this wise, young lady? He's a violent criminal.'

'I want to forget this ever happened.'

'You're making a big mistake, my dear.' He gave her a standard form to sign. She went outside and waited in the rain for a taxi; but she couldn't go back to Mandy's after all that had happened.

## CHAPTER 16

Going back to Stephen's felt a bit like going home. He wasn't alone — a prostitute sat at the kitchen table in suspenders and black corset.

'Hi,' she said. 'I'm Ronna.'

Within a few days Lucky was back. Each night he watched from the street. He saw who came and went; he saw the lights in the flat go on and off. Christine never spoke to him.

'You must have it out,' said Stephen.

She went back to the El Rio Café, where Lucky sat drinking cold coffee, and ordered a refill. He looked so helpless, she felt sorry for him.

'I'm sorry,' he croaked. 'I tried to let you go, but I can't.'

'I know.'

'I love you, Christine. Don't you feel the same?'

'Not when you're angry.'

'You'd love me more if I wasn't black.'

'That's not true.' She sighed. What did it matter how she felt? It was what other people thought that counted.

Lucky nodded. 'Have you ever been in love?'

'Of course.' She thought of Manu, the Persian student she'd been with while working at the Cabaret Club. They'd fallen out after she moved in with Stephen. Then there was Noel, Stephen's friend. But he'd left her high and dry.

'I'd like to take you home to meet my mother. You'll see how good it could be. We can be happy, Christine. We'll go there now, it isn't far.'

She let him hold her hand. Why not meet his mother? She was feeling curious, and it had to be better than going back to Stephen.

~

'Christine, where have you been?' She kicked off her shoes. Stephen was tidying up. 'I've been taking your messages like a secretary. Your mother's worried, and Mandy ...'

'Mandy?' She had forgotten Mandy existed.

'Yes, she's back. Name-dropping like you wouldn't believe; of course I'm not impressed. She's been working for Robert Mitchum, taking care of his affairs ... and they're complicated. He smokes more dope than you do.'

Christine yawned, and took off her coat. 'She didn't stay over? I went to see Lucky. We've sorted everything out.' Stephen raised an eyebrow. 'We went to his mum's; I didn't see much of her though.'

Stephen lined up a box of dominoes on the table. 'Didn't I tell you not to encourage him?'

Her temper flared. 'Well, I had to do something. You wouldn't get off my back!'

Stephen made no reply. He tipped the dominoes and they fell.

'Why did you do that?' she protested. 'I wanted to play.'

He put on his spectacles and lit up a cigarette. 'You'll never get shot of Lucky now. I despair of you sometimes, Christine. I should wash my hands of you. Can you make yourself scarce, please? Eugene will be here soon.'

## CHAPTER 17

'How long have you been here, my dear?'
'Oh — not long. But I've been on the game since I left school.'
Ronna Riccardo got out of bed, slung on a frayed silk robe and helped herself to one of Stephen's cigarettes. She liked working at her flat on Dolphin Square. Ten minutes' walk from the Houses of Parliament, it attracted a better class of city gent; rich, and easily satisfied.

Stephen counted three pounds from his wallet, and she accepted it with a grin. 'I shall come again, maybe next week,' he said. 'I'll give you my telephone number — if you ever need to see me, call after seven.' He copied it onto a scrap of pink tissue, and went.

As he walked downstairs, a man blocked his way. 'Well, if it isn't you, Ward. Fancy us meeting in a place like this!' John Lewis had crossed Stephen's path years before; his wife, Joy, had come to Stephen as a patient. He introduced her to a woman in his waiting room, and Joy left Lewis soon after.

'Actually,' said Stephen, 'it's just the sort of place I'd expect to see you in. Are you following me, Lewis?' Eight years ago, Lewis leaked a rumour to the *Daily Express* that Stephen was running a brothel in Mayfair; but the editor, also a patient of Stephen's, prevented it from going to print.

Ronna poked her head out of the door. 'Hey, keep your voices down or my landlord will have you both chucked out!'

Lewis brushed past Stephen, knocking on a door adjacent to Ronna's. 'I could have you followed day and night if I wanted to. But why bother? Your days are numbered, Ward.'

Stephen left without giving a reply. He got into his car which was parked a couple of streets away, lit up a cigarette and drove towards Soho. A blonde came out of a pub on Tottenham Court Road. He waved and stopped the car.

She was pale and scrawny, not really his type. He rolled down the window anyway, and she leaned in. 'Why don't you go back in there and buy me a bottle of sherry?' He passed her two guineas. She returned with a brown paper bag, and no change; he opened the car door. 'Let's go to my place and drink this together,' he said, as she slumped on the back seat.

'Cheers,' she replied, unscrewing the bottle and taking a swig. 'By the way, I'm Vickie — pleased to meet you, sir.'

## CHAPTER 18

Christine took the gun from her drawer and put it in her handbag. She'd got it in a pub on the Old Kent Road, from an Austrian man named Carl. Paula knew him. Paula was one of her new friends. Kim and Nina were others.

A taxi waited outside. (She drove everywhere since Lucky surprised her one day. She'd come out of the hairdresser's and was on her way to lunch when he jumped her in the street, knocked her to the ground. No one helped, shoppers looked aghast. 'Bitch!' he shouted, spitting on her. Then he hopped on a bus, left her lying there.)

She paid the driver in change, and rang the bell for Paula's flat. Paula was thinner than Christine, and her hair was a darker red. Unlike Mandy, she smoked. She knew who sold the best grass.

Christine opened her purse and proudly showed off her new gun to Paula and a man called Johnny.

'What do you want a gun for?' he teased. 'A nice girl like you.'

Paula tutted, and passed the joint to Christine.

'A man is following me.' Christine slumped into a yellow armchair. 'His name is Lucky. Have you met him?'

'Sure I have.' Johnny smiled.

'Do you know how he got his name?' Paula said. 'He broke out of prison three times in Jamaica — then he skipped the country.'

'I'm from Kingston too.' Johnny put an arm around Christine, who was shaking.

'He's mad about her,' Paula explained. 'He sleeps outside her house.'

Johnny adjusted his hat, and rolled a fresh joint. 'You need a man to take care of you. I'll get rid of him, Christine.'

~

Eugene parked on the kerb outside Stephen's surgery, hurried past reception. Stephen's rooms were painted green and purple. He pulled down the blind, flicked on a lamp.

'Drinks, old man?' Stephen opened a cabinet of spirits, gifts from his patients, choosing an evil-smelling liqueur.

'Just leave the bottle on the table.' Eugene drained his glass. 'Any news?'

'I'm waiting for Godfrey to ring.' Stephen shook his head. He looked tired. 'It's deadly serious. America will strike at Cuba unless Russia backs off. There could be another world war — a nuclear war.'

'Khrushchev will go all the way.' Eugene trusted his stocky leader. 'Our ships will not turn back.'

'But the missile sites the Soviets are building — surely Kennedy is right to intervene? Mr Khrushchev has no right to put them there.'

'And what right does John Kennedy have to invade the Caribbean?' Eugene banged his fist on the fragile trestle table. 'Castro will stand the test of time. With a little help from us, he'll bring Marx to all the Americas.'

'Yes, but it may come too late ... for humanity, I mean.'

Eugene laughed. 'So the people must pay the price. All this could be avoided if the English would only act. And Stephen, you know so many people, important people ... men like us can change the world. You must use your influence in this matter. With the English on our side, Kennedy will not dare to start a war, and we shall both be heroes.'

Stephen's eyes were open, awake. 'You really think we can do that, Eugene?'

~

'See?' Christine pointed and whispered. 'That's Lucky Gordon, over there.' Johnny spat on the floor and pulled down his trilby a notch. Lucky was on the other side of the club with his brothers. He usually came alone. He was laughing and joking, pretending not to notice Christine with another man.

Lucky and Johnny knew each other all right. They'd come to London from Kingston at about the same time. They'd both worked briefly at the East India docks. Last summer Lucky played cards and drunk beer on the steps of Johnny's pad in Kilburn. Then Johnny moved to the Grove and stole Lucky's pitch.

'Give me your gun,' Johnny whispered to Christine. She took it reluctantly from her brown leather handbag.

Johnny walked past the tables of white people wining and dining, the centre of the All-Nighter. She followed behind lamely until they reached the small group by the opposite wall. Conversation stopped and Lucky stared, the smile fleeing his face.

'What's up, Lucky?' Johnny grinned.

Lucky shrugged. 'Nothing. Why're you here?'

'I'm really going places now, Lucky. I'm here tonight with my girlfriend, Christine.' Johnny gripped her shoulder. 'When I come here the man shows me to a good table. I ain't treated like no nigger, my man.'

'What's going on?' Lucky kept his eyes on Christine. 'You're supposed to be my girl.'

'She's mine now, all mine.' Johnny's grip tightened. 'She's too beautiful for you, you creepy freak.'

Lucky grabbed the strap on Christine's dress. She jumped back, shielding her head from the gunfire she expected. But there was no sound, just one silent slash across Lucky's face.

The party broke up in screams and she ran. 'Get out of here!' The doorman pushed her onto the street. 'Don't come back!' She swung round and Johnny was there, buttoning his jacket.

'You were going to leave me there, weren't you?' He wiped blood off his knife. 'You won't get rid of me that easily. We're in this together now.'

She dove blindly after him into a car. 'Liverpool Street Station,' he told the driver. 'I've got relatives in Essex. We'll go there for a few days, until this thing blows over. Don't worry, Christine.'

He wrapped his arm round her. She shuddered. Cold rain danced down the highway.

## CHAPTER 19

The curtains were drawn as the afternoon turned dark. Mandy put the gas fire on and slumped on Stephen's sofa. She was re-reading *Gone With the Wind*, a book she had loved the first time round. It didn't seem that gripping anymore. She reached for the bottle of brandy she'd found in the kitchen, but it was empty.

Just a fortnight ago Peter had dropped dead. It was a heart attack and he died instantly. It was Stephen who told her, and invited her to stay. One night she swallowed a handful of pills, intending to follow Peter. But Christine had found her, and she was grateful to her for that.

Christine joined her with a pot of tea and some scones she had baked. She laid the tray down while Mandy made room for her on the sofa.

'I've been on the phone to a letting agent,' she told Mandy. 'We can go and look at a flat tomorrow, if you like ... two bedrooms, and it's on Cumberland Place.' The lease on Stephen's flat was due to expire in December, and he wanted to find something smaller.

Mandy sighed. She hadn't been back to Bryanston Mews since Peter died. It was all she had left of him, as he hadn't included her in his will.

Stephen walked in, threw his coat over an armchair, and grabbed one of Christine's scones. 'Good grief, Mandy, aren't you dressed yet? You look terrible.'

'I feel it,' she whimpered. 'My period's due, and I've had the most dreadful headache all day. Won't you give me an aspirin?'

He knelt by the sofa and held her face in his hands, rubbing his fingers across her forehead and down to the nape of her neck. Christine poured three fresh cups of tea.

'I'm meeting a friend for lunch tomorrow,' Stephen continued. 'I want you to come with me, Mandy. He's called Emil — Emil Savundra. He's a doctor from Burma. It will do you good to get out and about — and besides, he's filthy rich.'

~

A fire burned at Spring Cottage. The pheasant was eaten. Stephen and Bill shared a second bottle of rosé, while Eugene battered his nerves with vodka. The crockery stewed in the sink. Stephen adjusted the aerial as his television set crackled into life.

He twiddled the volume but no sound came. Khrushchev and Kennedy were shaking hands. Khrushchev hugged his rival, Kennedy's face touching the old man's purple cheeks. "Peace has come to Cuba," an Englishman's voice broke in. "Agreement has been reached."

Eugene dropped his glass. It smashed to pieces. He stood up.

'I ... don't understand.' His voice teetered on the brink of rage. 'Why has he given in to that playboy? We almost had it made.'

Bill leaned towards him and frowned. 'But surely this is wonderful news. The world was close to extinction.'

Eugene shrugged. He could think of nothing but the humiliation of Russia. He turned away.

'Stephen, could I have done any more to bring our two nations together?'

Stephen smiled meekly, embarrassed for his friend. 'Eugene, we played our part, and it has all worked out for the best.'

Bill chuckled. 'Gentlemen, this is no matter for a couple of back-door diplomats. We Brits were always on the American side; you Cossacks didn't stand a chance.'

'Khrushchev won't go away empty-handed.' Eugene shook his head. 'Castro will never cave in to America. Stephen, I must be going. I'll drive to the embassy before it's too late.' He went into the garden and lit up a cigar, wishing he were anywhere but in England.

## CHAPTER 20

Mandy set her hair in rollers and sat on the bed, waiting to curl. She played with the ribbon on her pink flannel robe. Christine held a hand mirror and doused her free hand in a tub of Pond's, slapping it over her face.

The telephone rang. Neither girl moved.

'Good thing I'm leaving here,' Christine said. 'I never know who might be calling nowadays. It could be Lucky ... or Johnny.' She'd avoided Johnny since their weekend in Billericay, after the knifing. He still had her gun.

'Pass me the mirror, will you?' Mandy sighed. 'I'll never understand you, Christine. You could have any man in London, yet you picked him.' She grimaced at her reflection. 'Anyway, wasn't Lucky here just the other day?'

'Yes, he brought me his stitches.' Christine forced a laugh. 'He dropped them through the letterbox. There were seventeen, I counted them — Stephen says they look like ants.'

'We'll have to hurry if we're to move our things today,' said Mandy. 'I haven't even started packing my clothes.' The lease on their new flat had begun two days ago. 'I've got speeches to learn for my acting class.'

'I thought you'd given all that up?'

'Emil's helping out until I get another job. He's a gentleman — very discreet.'

The doorbell rang. 'Don't get it,' said Christine. 'We can't be seen half-dressed.' A moment later, it buzzed again. She nudged Mandy. 'Go to the window. See who it is.'

Mandy peeped out. 'Christine — it's a coloured man. He's wearing a hat — it must be Johnny Edgecombe.' A stone hit the window.

'Oh, tell him to get lost.' Christine tensed up and smiled stiffly.

'Christine!' Johnny shouted. 'Christine!' A taxi driver waited, watching the meter. Net curtains were raised and a neighbour peered out of her front door.

Mandy opened the window slightly. 'Christine's not here. You'll have to — *um* — try again.'

'You're a lying cow!' He pulled Christine's gun from his pocket and pointed at Mandy, who jumped away. She crawled to the telephone.

'What are you doing?' Christine squealed, and covered her mouth.

'We'll have to get help. I'll call the police — or Stephen, or somebody.'

'Don't you dare tell Stephen! He'll blame me, as usual. It's no good — I'll have to talk to Johnny.'

'Let me in, Christine!' he yelled from the street. 'Or I'll kill you both.'

'Don't be stupid, Johnny!' She moved towards the window. 'Look — you're causing a scene. We can talk about it somewhere else. Here —' she threw a pound note down to him — 'meet me at the El Rio.' Johnny spat on the note as it landed and fired two shots at the front door.

Christine hid under the bed as the shooting continued. Mandy dialled Stephen's surgery and a nurse called out the police. Johnny, spotting the small crowd that had gathered, gave up and got into the cab.

'Take me back to Brentford, mate.' The cabbie revved up the car.

~

The police finished questioning Mandy and Christine after seven. They had arrested Johnny at his flat, and locked him in a cell. Outside Marylebone station was a cluster of men who Mandy guessed were reporters. She took out her powder puff, but they had already spotted Christine.

'I'm from the *Mirror*.' A man offered his hand. 'Miss Keeler, isn't it?'

'How do you know?' A flashbulb went off and another man pulled on her sleeve. Mandy smiled and adjusted her hat, but Christine froze.

'You did that swimsuit page for us last summer, remember? You're a lovely little model — one of my favourites. Come and see me sometime. You can tell me about that M.P. friend of yours ... there's money in it for you.'

The men surged forward. Mandy was hailing a cab. 'I know about the letter!' the journalist shouted. Christine dived in after Mandy, trembling.

'Wimpole Mews, please —'

'No, not there. Stephen will be home any minute. Let's go to our new flat. Cumberland Place!' she called through the hatch.

'What's the matter, Christine? You're all out of breath.' Mandy gave her clean handkerchief to Christine, who was crying.

'Leaving Stephen like this. After all he's done for me.'

'But he's going too.' Stephen was taking Mandy's flat at Bryanston Mews, which was close to his surgery. 'You can still be friends. Anyway,' she added slyly, 'he gets more peculiar by the day. Really, aren't you glad to be rid of him?'

'That's not true!' Christine blew her nose. 'He introduced me to some very important people. I'll be a famous model one day.' She had work lined up for the new year, modelling hats. 'Soon I'll be able to pay off my debts.'

Mandy paid the driver and Christine tipped him. They stood silently for a moment outside their new block. Christine hugged Mandy impulsively.

'Won't it be brilliant, us living together? You're right. Stephen was far too old.' They went in. Mandy fished out the keys. Their flat was empty except for a wooden chair that faced the window. She sat down.

'What happened just now — the press and everything. It *was* about Johnny, wasn't it?'

'Of course.' Christine lit up a cigarette. 'Why else would they want to talk to me? I expect there'll be a trial.'

'It'll be all over the papers. I don't want any scandal, Christine.'

'It'll blow over. Where's the phone?'

'We're not connected yet.' Mandy looked up as Christine walked out, leaving the door on the latch.

Christine was agitated. She found a public callbox and dialled Michael Eddowes, a friend of Stephen's. He was a retired solicitor. She knew she could trust him; he always knew what to do.

# CHAPTER 21

'Excuse me miss. Aren't you the girl who got shot at last week?'

Christine glanced up from her punch glass. The man speaking was short and fat and wore an ill-fitting suit. He seemed harmless enough. She nodded wearily.

'What an ordeal for you. No doubt you'll be called upon in court?'

'I'd avoid it if I could. I don't want the publicity.' Each morning she was woken by reporters, who stayed on her doorstep all day.

'I'm John Lewis.' The man sat uncomfortably close. 'You can't believe what you read in the papers — I recently sued for a quarter million.'

She downed her drink; it tasted awful. She accepted a cigar. It was a quiet party, for Christmas Eve. She wished she had gone to her mum's.

'If you're looking for advice — or representation — I have an excellent solicitor. Maybe we could talk elsewhere? I'm going back to St. John's Wood now.'

She let him help her into the chinchilla jacket she'd borrowed from Mandy. 'It might be worth it,' she thought. 'I need all the help I can get.'

~

She lit a fire in John Lewis's parlour, which was filled with antiques. The bookshelves were lined with almanacs. He opened a French cognac; she could see he was used to drinking.

'That's my office in there.' He pointed to a door in the wall. 'I keep files on all kinds of people.' He stared down her dress.

'Is that part of your job?'

He laughed. 'I'm a Labour man. I was in Attlee's government. But I made my money in rubber.'

She folded her arms. He nuzzled her bare shoulder.

'I need someone to defend me,' she said. 'I don't want my past getting dragged up in court.'

'Your past?' He smirked.

'Yes — Johnny, and Lucky. I don't want to talk about my sex life. I don't want anyone to know I've slept with a black man. It's not that I mind — it's my family who'll suffer. I come from a very small town.'

'The prosecution will make you tell everything. You have a case to answer. If you don't tell the whole truth, they'll sue you for perjury.' He slipped his hand under her skirt. 'That's why you must tell me — now. You're one of Ward's girls, aren't you? The old ponce.'

She pushed him away. 'Stephen is my friend. What has this got to do with him?'

'He procured you for Jack Profumo — and Eugene Ivanov. It's been the talk of London for months. The jury will want to know if he's been keeping prostitutes.'

'I'm not a whore. Jack never gave me anything — except a lighter once, and a bottle of perfume.'

'Ward set you up with Profumo and Ivanov to find out about the bomb. Everyone knows he's a spy.'

'That's a lie. I hardly knew Jack at all. And I only slept with Eugene once — that doesn't make us lovers.'

John Lewis leered. 'You whores are all the same — you're all in love with your ponces. He chucked you out, didn't he? You can't afford to be proud anymore.'

She got up, grabbed her coat, and pulled the door open. 'I'll see Ward hang for this,' he said. 'He deserves it — he wrecked my marriage. You'll be back when your friends run out on you.'

She was gone. He switched off the tape recorder he kept behind the Chesterfield sofa, went to the telephone and dialled his old party colleague, George Wigg. 'I've got a lead for you,' he chuckled. 'Sort of a Christmas bonus ...'

## CHAPTER 22
## 1963

Eugene and Stephen walked through Hyde Park, sharing a flask of brandy. The park was deserted and covered with snow, and fog wafted through the air.

'I've never known such cold,' Stephen shivered. 'It has brought the city to a standstill.' Temperatures had dropped to below zero. Railway tracks were frozen, cars had crashed and were left abandoned on the streets.

'In Russia it is quite normal; we can survive these winters. You English are not so well prepared.' They walked on, trudging through the snow. Stephen was unusually quiet.

'I have been called back to Moscow,' Eugene continued. 'It's my mother ... she is very ill.' She had cancer of the throat, but that was only half the truth; a scandal was breaking in London that could expose him as a spy, and would certainly destroy Stephen, Christine and Jack Profumo.

'I'm so sorry.' Stephen wished he could have done more for Eugene, who had promised him a better life in Russia.

Eugene took a slug of brandy and let it burn his throat. 'What will you do now, Steve?'

Stephen shrugged. 'Carry on as usual, I suppose. I'll try to be a good doctor and keep out of trouble. I envy you reds, you know. I've never had your passion or your convictions. I've always just drifted along, hoping to find my purpose on the way — but it hasn't happened yet.'

'What about Christine? She thinks the world of you.'

'She's too young for me. We're not equals — we don't understand each other.'

Eugene sighed. 'It is a great pity. I like living among the English. I've made many good contacts. I had plans for us ... but it has all come to nothing.'

They reached the park gates. Stephen's voice faltered. 'I shall miss you, Eugene. I won't forget your generosity.' The two men embraced, and Eugene hurried away.

'Take care of yourself!' Stephen shouted, but Eugene didn't hear. The roads were knee-deep in filth and snow. He walked back to the surgery, choked up and wishing he could escape.

## CHAPTER 23

Stephen joined Bill Astor and Jack Profumo as arranged, in a suite at Claridge's on a cold, wet Thursday in January. The rooms were decorated cream and gold. Chairs were cushioned and lamps gave a warm light.

'Gentlemen, there is no easy way to say this — the boys from Fleet Street have got us in a spot of bother.' Bill, plump and stately, circled the two men who sat smoking cigars by an open fire. Profumo looked pale and ill at ease.

Bill looked out of the window, through the nets to the hailstones that beat hard. 'Something's brewing — something dreadful — and we may all be dragged into it. I've been scouting about these last few days, and it appears your friend Christine has gone to the papers.'

He turned and faced Stephen.

'But why should this concern me? I haven't heard from Christine since she moved out.' He had not returned her messages. 'She's completely scatter-brained, definitely not to be trusted.' He looked nervously to the wall.

'We've got to shut her up,' Bill replied. 'She's been talking to everyone about you ... Jack ... and Ivanov. There's no predicting who else she'll drag into this sordid affair — and I won't let my family name go through the mud.'

'How much is she getting?' Jack asked.

'I'm not sure — maybe a thousand. She's worth a lot more than that to us. She's going to court next week over that shooting business with Mr Edgecombe; who knows what the silly girl will say then? Our reputations on the line with gangsters, drugs and tarts?'

'Just mischievous gossip from a young girl.' Stephen stirred his tea. 'I don't imagine anyone will take her seriously.'

Bill sighed. 'Stephen, I do suggest you contact your counsel. There are people who are out to get you for this. It might be expensive — I can lend you the money.'

Jack stood up as if to go. 'I should have known you were trouble, Ward!' He stayed by the door.

'There's a rumour,' Bill continued, 'that you've been introducing your patients to girls, and charging them for it, and living off the earnings of those girls.'

'But that's rubbish! No one will believe that! Who in their right mind would say such a thing?' Stephen shook his head, laughing, incredulous. 'After all, I'm a doctor, I don't need the money.'

'You've hardly been careful, Stephen. You've made a lot of enemies. And you've left yourself open to all kinds of allegations.'

Jack walked out, slamming the door, and then came back again. 'You're nothing but a jumped-up ponce, Ward! How dare you set me up like this! If this is true, I'll see you rot in jail before you sabotage my career. I could be Prime Minister ...' His voice cracked. He made a dash for the lift.

Bill patted Stephen on the head. 'Not to worry, old man. Probably a storm in a teacup. We'll pay off Christine, and the whole thing will be forgotten.'

'I didn't mean for this to happen. I won't let them destroy you, Bill. Or Jack. You are my dearest friend.'

'You could ask her to leave the country,' Bill suggested. 'Just for a short time, until we put a lid on all this.'

Stephen sighed. 'It's not safe for me to talk to her — you never know who may be listening. But maybe someone else could ask on our behalf. Paul Mann's a good friend of hers, and mine.'

'I know you won't turn your back on us.' Bill reached for his waistcoat. 'And I won't let you down. Come on, Steve. Let's go downstairs and get drunk.'

Stephen followed Bill blindly. His plans for Christine were forever ruined, and now she would turn against him. But he didn't blame the girl entirely. Though he loved her like an indulgent father, he had long since thrown her to the wolves.

~

Christine sat in her overcoat, smoking the reporter's cigarettes. A bottle of malt whiskey, a notepad and pencil and a typewriter stood between them. He drummed his fingers on the table while she studied his dirty fingernails.

'I do hope you've written it up for me. I'm not very good with words.'

'Certainly, darling.' He passed her the proofs. 'Why don't you read it? You can *read*, can't you?'

She glared briefly at him and began. "Men are such fools," she repeated. "But I like them. I have always liked them." She laughed. It didn't sound like her or anyone she'd met. They had turned her into a character from a bad film — the other woman.

She finished the article quickly and handed it back to the reporter. 'I never thought I'd be doing this, not in a million years. Can I have another drink?' The reporter shrugged. 'Ratting on people, getting paid for it ...'

'You're pleased with our little story, then?'

'Oh yes. It's quite all right. Mandy says it will be good publicity. I suppose I don't have a choice.' (She was broke again, and the agency had dropped her. Mr Eddowes refused to represent her, and reported her phonecall to another tabloid. Old friends like Michael Lambton were too busy to see her, while Major Jim wasn't due leave until spring. She had sold her fur coat to another model, Kim.)

'Mandy? She's the young lady you live with, isn't she?'

'We used to work at Murray's.'

'And what about that doctor you're so keen on? You two were close for a while.'

'I'm not keen on him. Not anymore. I want him kept out of it.'

The reporter chewed on his pencil, then stuck it behind his ear. 'You've got to save your own skin, my dear. I happen to know your Dr Ward has been talking to Mr Profumo. They've been calling us every day — they want to shut you up for good.'

Christine gulped down her scotch, and stared at the naked bulb that dangled from the ceiling. The light was harsh and the room, with its bundles of foolscap piled in no particular order, seemed to close in on her. She wanted this business to be over, and to go home on her own.

'So,' she said finally. 'What can I tell you about Stephen?'

# CHAPTER 24

Valerie wasn't surprised; she knew Jack liked young women, and he was used to getting what he wanted. Three anonymous letters had been sent, telling her of an affair with a girl named Christine Keeler. Jack said they had come from MI5. It was cowardly of them, she thought.

She poured tea with a steady hand. Jack sat across the table, winding up his gold wristwatch. He never seemed comfortable in his own home. The window showed blackness and snow. It was just before seven.

'I'm afraid our lives will be difficult for a time. Thank God I have you to fall back on.'

She nodded. A few years ago she had been an actress, but she knew her worth as a wife. He needed her now — he knew he could trust her. And the last thing she wanted was another messy divorce.

'The children love you dearly, darling. Tell me about the girl.'

'There's not much to say. She's uneducated, not well off. She's asking for five thousand.'

'Then why don't you give it to her? She could have asked for so much more.'

'I won't be blackmailed.' Jack went red. 'I've half a mind to sue.'

'I'm sorry, darling. She'll back down, you'll see. Surely the men from the intelligence services could help you — not to mention the party. It's a matter of honour.'

'The secret service have washed their hands of me. They don't want to get mixed up in it. It was MI5 who recruited Ward — it's all his fault. He foisted that girl on me. Bill Astor says he's friendly with the Russians; sympathetic to their cause. Eugene Ivanov's a crony of his.'

'That handsome captain? I rather liked him.' Jack brushed past her into the hall, smearing a kiss on her forehead. She heard him pick up his overcoat and his umbrella. She imagined him adjusting his scarf and hat. He slammed the door and left the house, revved up the Daimler and drove through the gates.

# CHAPTER 25

'My name is Christine Keeler. I'm the missing model you heard about. I've come to give myself up.'

The clerk looked up from his desk. The girl held up a copy of that morning's *Express*. She was pictured on the front page, above the headline, "VANISHED." An article about the war minister John Profumo's alleged affair with a showgirl sat opposite.

'We've been looking for you, Miss Keeler. Who brought you here?'

'Nobody. I came with my friends, Kim and Paul.'

'You have broken the law, young lady. You were summonsed to Marylebone Crown Court, for the trial of John Edgecombe. You were a witness for the prosecution.'

'I'm sorry. I was frightened.' A gang of British and American reporters waited for her at the door of the British Consul. 'Some men are threatening me. One of them is Lucky Gordon ... he wants to cut me up.'

The clerk shrugged. 'Evading trial is a serious misdemeanour. In any case, Mr. Edgecombe has been sentenced to seven years' imprisonment.'

'For defending me?' Christine gasped. 'I thought he'd be let off if I wasn't there.' Maybe Lucky's brothers were right — British justice didn't apply to black men. The trial might even have been fixed. She shouldn't have dragged Johnny into it.

'Why did you come to Spain?' the clerk asked. 'Where have you been staying?'

'It was Paul's idea, I suppose. I needed a break.' It had been a rotten holiday; hiding out in a village on the coast, playing monotonous games of bridge. She'd hoped Spain would be hotter in March than London, but she hadn't a trace of a tan.

'Then we drove to Madrid for the bullfight. That's when I got recognised. We don't have any money. Paul's going to cash his insurance policy.' She looked desperate. 'I've got nowhere to stay, and I need to phone my mother. I thought I'd be forgotten if I went away. It would be better if I was.'

'This friend of yours, Paul Mann. How did you meet him?'

'When I lived with Stephen — Doctor Ward.'

'Did Mr. Mann or Doctor Ward suggest you should leave the country?'

She shook her head. 'I told you, I wanted to go. I haven't seen Stephen since before Christmas. I met Kim at an audition on Charing Cross Road — she knows nothing about any of this. She and Paul only wanted to help me.'

'Dr Ward gave an interview to the *Sunday Pictorial* about your friendship with Mr Profumo. He says you're planning to sell your own story.'

'He turned his back on me. I had to do something. My interview hasn't been published yet.'

'You must fly back to London immediately. The police will question you. There are rumours that your relationship with Mr Profumo was not altogether proper; people are saying you also slept with a Russian man.'

'I'll tell the police the truth about Jack. I'll tell the newspapers too.' The *Express* had offered her two thousand pounds. Enough money to go on a long holiday, and to take care of mum and dad. If any good should come of this, they would live out their days in a house of their own. She told herself she wasn't afraid. Paul would stand by her, and together they'd strike up a deal with the press.

~

Dawn broke. Valerie stood, dusted the Persian blue off her lap and drew back the curtains. From the kitchen window she could see the last car turn around the bend, as in a funeral procession. The morning's first light was bleak. She set water to boil on the Aga, for another pot of coffee as the front door quietly closed and her husband's footsteps approached.

He sat down in a wooden chair, pulled on a red cardigan. The stone floor was cold. He smiled gratefully as she placed a mug in his hand. The hangdog expression was familiar by now, and it didn't convince. This was not the man she had married; she looked quickly away.

'I will speak to the House today. The party has drafted a statement, everything has been arranged.' She nodded as he passed her the typed memorandum.

"My wife and I first met Miss Keeler at a house party in July 1961, at Cliveden ... I met Miss Keeler on about half a dozen occasions at Dr Ward's flat when I called to see him ... There was no impropriety whatsoever in my acquaintance with Miss Keeler ..."

Valerie folded the stiff sheet of paper and placed it in her lap. 'It's a very strong statement, dear. I'm sure no one will doubt your intentions. But I can't help wondering — wouldn't it be wiser to admit your mistake? Then both our consciences will be clear.'

Jack's eyes narrowed. 'Darling, you're wonderfully naive. It would be beneath me to take such a risk with all our futures. You do understand, my dear?'

'Of course.' Her lips pursed. She was close to anger, but he wouldn't let up.

'I won't be coming home after question time. But there's a charity dinner tonight at Quaglino's and I do hope you'll accompany me. It is so important that we put up a united front.'

'I'll be there.' She composed herself. 'It will be nice to go out together again. You've been so busy lately.' She dangled the denial in her hand. 'I must find myself something to wear. Shall I put it on the account, dear?'

## CHAPTER 26

Stephen woke with a start. The pillow beside him was sunken, the blankets turned over. The alarm clock said twenty past one. He'd been at the pub on the corner all night. He didn't remember coming home. In the days when he lived with Christine, they would stay up and talk about what had gone on. Light leaked in from the kitchen.

'Hello? Who's there?' He must have brought somebody back with him, but he hadn't seen Ronna for a couple of weeks; hadn't picked up anyone in his car since that time with Vickie.

A blonde came into the bedroom, in black suspenders and kitten heels. Her roots were showing. 'Don't you remember me, darling?' She spoke with a nasal twang. She sat with him on the bed, swigging claret from the bottle. 'I like a drink after work.'

'I'm sorry. You are ...'

'Wendy. From the Duke of Marlborough, down the road. You've not been living here long, have you?'

'No.' He spent as little time at home as he could manage, taking on extra clients and staying late at the surgery. There was no room for guests. He hated being alone, ending most evenings drunk and confused. Eugene was gone, and Christine hated him. Even Mr Hollis wouldn't return his calls.

'Wendy, Wendy,' he said. 'It's so nice of you to come. I have a superb cognac, given to me by a dear friend from Russia. Won't you join me in a toast?'

She lifted her dress from the heap on the carpet, and pulled it over her head. 'I think I'm just about done here, mister. Come and see me tomorrow? Behind the bar, I mean.'

'You'll be there, will you?' He dug into his wallet, and gave her his last five-pound note, wondering where the money went.

'All day, every day except Wednesday afternoon.' She blew him a kiss, her lips stained dark red. He watched her from the window. She went into the telephone box and dialled, looking up at him like prey. He wondered whom she could be speaking to at this hour.

In the cramped study his desk was open and his correspondence laid out. It was nonsense, of course, to suppose she had been reading it. His drinks cabinet was also open and emptier than he calculated.

He picked out the Gordon's gin, took it into the kitchen. He poured some into a white mug, cracked an egg and stirred the yolk in. He drank. Then he poured another, straight this time, and went to the bathroom. He fished out some pills from the medicine box and swallowed.

~

'It's good of you to spare me five minutes, doctor.'

Stephen tensed up. He wouldn't allow the man to see him scared.

'Stella?' His receptionist looked apologetic. 'I'm fully booked this morning. I asked you not to disturb me.'

'It's not the lady's fault.' The detective smiled. 'This is a police matter.'

'Well, at least bring up some coffee and biscuits. I must have coffee — it's ten past eleven.' The receptionist nodded. She looked as nervous as he felt.

'Business going well, sir?' The detective said as she left.

'You could say that. Now look here, inspector. If this is about Mr Profumo — '

'You've got something to tell us, then?'

'Only that I want no more to do with this affair. I've risked my reputation to protect Mr Profumo, as any friend would.'

'Forgive me doctor, but you sound rather on edge.' The receptionist knocked and brought in a tray. Stephen smiled gratefully as she went and drank a cup. The detective eyed the wafers and bourbons.

'It's not that I've been telling lies, but in doing my best for others, I've been put in a compromising position.'

'So what's it all about, doctor? What are you trying to say?'

'I've done all I can for everyone involved in this enquiry. When I found Christine with Mr Ivanov, I warned Mr Profumo because I knew Ivanov would take advantage. I even telephoned MI5. It was I who saw the danger — the danger for our country.'

'What danger, Doctor Ward? Isn't this rather far-fetched?'

'Christine got mixed up with an English minister — and a Russian spy. One would go out the door and another would come in. Ivanov wanted to pump secrets out of her — he told me as much. He may even have asked her himself.'

'Was she working for him, do you think?'

'Maybe you should ask her. I haven't seen her since she moved away — I haven't spoken to her all year.'

'You see, I've been making my own enquiries,' the detective replied. 'I've spoken to MI5 and they've never heard of you, doctor. They have no record of ever having dealt with you. And there are no cabinet files on this security breach you keep talking about.'

'There must be some mistake,' said Stephen. 'It was they who approached me. I know there's a dossier somewhere on all this. It may be lost — we must find it.'

'It's not for us to decide, doctor. The courts will make a report — Lord Denning's in charge of government affairs. It will all be tidied up nicely.'

'I'm sorry inspector, but I simply must get on. I've got patients waiting, and we seem to be getting nowhere.'

The detective stood up. 'Very well, sir. I shall need to speak to Miss Keeler again; you'll be hearing from us shortly.'

Stephen let him go without saying goodbye, and wondered what the police really wanted. He had written to the Prime Minister and the Home Secretary, telephoned MI5, and at each turn he was rebuffed. Only Harold Wilson, leader of the opposition, wanted to know. The Labour Party would listen, but it was one of their own — John Lewis — who had got him into this.

He blamed Christine for opening her mouth. He searched his pockets — he was out of cigarettes.

## CHAPTER 27

They'd been on a short trip to Venice, enjoying dinner in their hotel room when the telegram came. It was from Harold Macmillan's private secretary, asking them to return. Jack didn't want to; they were having such a nice time.

'We must go home and face it,' said Valerie.

He telephoned Mr Bligh. Neither mentioned any girl. Harold Wilson had contacted Mr Macmillan about a security matter involving Mr Profumo and Eugene Ivanov; there had been an indiscretion, and the story had gone to the *Sunday People*.

'You must come back in case it goes to print,' said Mr Bligh.

Valerie booked places for them both on boat and train that night. Mr Bligh met Jack at Dover, while Valerie took a car to a friend's house in Suffolk. All their friends were behind them. ('How awful,' they sighed, 'to be hounded by a common tart.')

Valerie phoned the au-pair and sent for their son. Jack busied himself in London. It was Whit-Sunday.

Mr Bligh had drafted a statement of resignation, which Jack approved. 'It certainly is a pity,' they agreed.

'Poor Jack,' said Valerie to her friend. 'I imagined we'd make it right to the top. Still, it wasn't to be.'

Maybe now he'd spend more time at home.

It was announced on the six o'clock news. A prepared statement was read by Richard Dimbleby. "I said that there was no impropriety in this association. To my very deep regret I have to admit that this was not true ..."

~

'What's impropriety?' Christine asked Paula, as they watched the news on television.

'Having it away ... with someone you shouldn't.' She was staying at Paula's now. She moved from one friend to another. Mandy had thrown her out. She said it was about the rent, but Christine was up to date.

Earlier that day, she'd got into a fight with Paula's brother, John, who was a friend of Stephen's. He gave her a black eye, but she still fought back. Everyone wanted a slice of her fame, and yet she had next to nothing in the bank.

Paula slapped on red lipstick. She was rat-eyed, with straggly brown hair. 'Let's go out, shall we?' she said. Staying in made her jumpy. 'We can have chips for our tea.'

'Maybe we could go to Stephen's?' asked Christine. 'I'm worried about him. He's not looking after himself. The police have been sniffing around me all week, but I'm sure it's him they're after.'

Paula shook her head. 'I don't think it's a good idea. Stephen can take care of himself.'

'That's what mum says. I called him last week, and he wanted me to star in a film with him! Or write a book — about my life.'

There was a knock at the door. Paula looked out.

'It's those two guys I spoke to earlier — maybe they've got some blow. Shall I let them in?'

Christine nodded wearily.

The men were regulars at the All-Nighter, and curious about her. 'Did you make it up with Lucky?' the younger one asked. 'I heard Johnny Edgecombe got five years.'

Christine sighed as the other one passed her a joint. 'Lucky's been tailing me ever since I got back from Spain. He got pulled in the other day.'

'Everyone's talking about it,' Paula grinned. 'She'll be rolling in money soon.'

'My article hasn't been printed yet.' Christine slipped into her shoes. 'I got two hundred pounds a month ago and not a penny since. It's my word against Jack Profumo's.'

'I feel sorry for him,' said Paula. 'His wife, his career ...'

'I've sold his letters to the *News of the World*. That'll teach him to make a fool out of me.'

They decided to go to the pub. As she opened the door, Lucky walked in. He pushed her against the wall and punched her face.

'Stephen said you'd be here!' He pushed her to the ground and kicked her in the ribs. The two men dragged him away from her. Paula dialled the police and Lucky ran.

Christine sat on a chair while Paula wiped blood from her eye.

'I can't believe they did this to you — Lucky and Stephen.'

'Stephen blames me for everything. He probably wants me out of the way.'

'Tell the police, and then take the money and run.'

'It's too late for that, Paula. I'm being set up, don't you see?'

The two men left quickly to avoid the police. Christine promised not to mention their names, or John's. She needed a place to stay, after all — and to be rid of Lucky for good. Minutes passed before the familiar faces of detectives Herbert and Burrows appeared.

Lucky was easily found. She agreed to press charges.

~

Stephen peeked through his bedroom curtain. He counted more than twenty pressmen waiting for him below. He recognised a few.

He dialled a few numbers from his well-worn address book, called people he hadn't seen in years. He needed to get out of London, but he wouldn't go to the cottage. He didn't want to embarrass the Astors.

At last he spoke to Bill Lang, a patient who produced films. They'd had lunch a week ago, and joked about making a film, to cash in on the scandal. Christine would play herself. They could sell it abroad, spice it up a bit.

Bill invited Stephen to his house near Watford. He packed a bag hurriedly, and greeted the press with a smile. ('Read all about it in the *News of the World*.') He got into the Jaguar he was so proud of. Bryanston Mews was jammed. He drove off in haste, just missing the car of an incoming journalist.

He drove through London, into Hertfordshire. Bill's wife had cooked for him. After dinner they talked of the future; he wanted to take a holiday. He slept soundly for seven hours, but was unsurprised the next morning when two policemen came to the house for him.

They took him back to London, where he was charged on nine counts of living off the wages of prostitution. The charges were spread over the last eighteen months. The women named included Mandy and Christine.

## CHAPTER 28

A cramped interview room was hidden at the back of Marylebone Police Station. John Burrows, the detective responsible for the Stephen Ward inquiry, led Commander Townsend of MI5 through the narrow, ill-lit corridors. He held the master key. He opened up the desk and took out a messy pile of cassettes, typescripts and memorandums.

The commander looked first at a detailed map of Profumo's house, drawn from Christine Keeler's description. It matched his set of photographs exactly.

'The girl has a long memory,' he said. 'She could be more of a threat than we thought.' The plan of Profumo's study interested him most.

John Burrows plugged in a tape recorder and played one of his interviews with Christine.

"Did Ward arrange for you to visit Mr Profumo at his home?"

"No — that was Jack's idea."

"Did Ward ask you to take anything from his study?"

"Of course not! Jack showed me his study, and then we went into the bedroom."

"Ivanov must have known about this. Did he offer you money to spy on Mr Profumo?"

There was a knock at the door and Sam Herbert, Burrows' partner, came in with a tray of drinks that he carried to the desk, dumping it on a sheaf of papers. He plonked himself on a chair and poured three glasses of scotch.

'None of this must get out,' the commander said. 'The merest hint of a spy ring could destroy our relations with America.'

'There's something else, sir — ' Burrows clicked the tape back on. 'Something Keeler said, here — '

"Eugene practically lived with us then, he seemed to be plotting something with Stephen. Then there were all those meetings with a man from MI5. Stephen made a joke; he asked me to find out from Jack when a bomb was going to be sent to West Germany by the Americans. He might have been serious, but I said no."

'You must burn this,' said Townsend. 'If it ever gets out, we're finished. There's got to be another way to get at Ward — he must be silenced.'

Burrows took a slug of whiskey, leaning back in his chair. There was no other dirt to pin on Ward that he knew of. Herbert played out a tape he had made with Mandy Rice-Davies, searching for something she had said.

"Do you like Ward, Mandy?"

"He's fun when you get to know him, but he's stingy."

"What about his sex life — does he have lots of girlfriends?"

"He likes having young girls in his flat, like Christine and me. I suppose we liven up the place. He was always bringing girls home when I was there, but he never introduced them to me."

"I've heard he likes orgies. Have you or Christine ever been to one with him?"

Herbert filled up his glass, knocking the ashtray off the desk with his elbow. Burrows hurriedly brushed up the cigarette ends while he told the commander, 'I've been talking to all the tarts from King's Cross and Soho; a girl called Ronna Riccardo says he used to be a punter of hers. She's terrified of me because I've had her up in court several times, and I'm sure she'll agree to name Ward as her ponce.'

'It sounds very promising, I must say. You must do whatever you think is necessary,' Commander Townsend said. 'With an attitude like yours, you'll go very far in the force.'

He left. Burrows lit up a cigarette.

'What's the matter, John?' Herbert took a squashed ham roll from his pocket, and stuffed it in his mouth. 'The trouble with you is you're too nice. I reckon you've got a crush on Keeler — pretty young thing like her ...'

'She's just a kid, Sam!'

'Then she's easy prey, so put the mockers on her. Listen John, you want to see that old ponce Ward locked up as much as I do, don't you?'

'Of course.'

'There are plenty of whores who'd be happy to help us do it for a few quid; and if a bribe doesn't work, we'll rustle up a soliciting charge. He's scum, mate, and she's no better. Anyway, are you in with me on this or do I have to go it alone?'

Burrows sighed. 'Like you said, Ward's scum, and he could be a traitor for all I know. Bring back the Riccardo bird, and any other tart you've found, then we'll stitch the bastard up for life.'

~

'Are you the defendant, Aloysius Gordon?'

'I am.' Lucky was on trial at Marylebone Crown Court after attacking Christine at Paula's house. He had sacked his solicitor the previous day and was representing himself. The witnesses, Christine and Paula, had been questioned, and Lucky was called by the judge to explain his actions.

'Christine is my girlfriend ... she cheated on me with Johnny Edgecombe. They followed me to the All-Nighter and he tried to kill me. I never hurt her although she asked for it many times. The doctor she lives with is a pimp, and she's nothing but a whore ... the lying bitch, she gave me VD — '

'He's lying — stop him!' She ran towards him and then froze as he was led away. The hearing was adjourned and the jury left to consider their verdict. She spotted Herbert and Burrows, the detectives investigating Stephen, conferring at the door. She hurried over. Herbert was doing a crossword; Burrows offered her a cigarette.

'Oh, inspector — this is the worst day of my life. I've never been so humiliated, and in front of so many people, I ...'

'Don't worry,' said Herbert. 'We've got hard evidence against him. He has lots of previous convictions and he won't get away with it this time.'

'Do you really think so?' It would be such a relief for the whole sorry business to be over. Stephen's trial was weeks away, and she was sure to be called as a witness. Lucky had called her a prostitute, and to her it felt like she was on trial and not him.

'Is something on your mind, Christine?' Burrows asked. Unlike Sam Herbert, who had bullied her and Mandy, John Burrows was a policeman she believed she could trust.

'There is one thing. When I told you about the persons present during the assault ...' She was thinking of Fenton and Commacchio, the two men whose names she had not mentioned in court, as promised. What would happen if they came forward now; would Lucky go free?

'Listen carefully, my girl, before you say something you might regret.' Herbert pulled her close, breathing down her neck. 'Nobody likes a man who hurts a woman, no matter what the provocation is. That judge will have him sent down for two or three years, so whatever you've got to say, it'll keep.'

Burrows touched her hand. 'He's right, Christine — you'll be safe as houses, you can rely on us.'

The jury returned a unanimous verdict after forty minutes, and Lucky was pronounced guilty of grievous bodily harm. As he was led away, he looked back at Christine. 'I'll get you for this!' he yelled, but his hands were chained.

# Chapter 29

It was Sunday, and the bedsits and boarding houses of Earl's Court were hardly stirring. Christine slept well, though not for long, on her new manager's sofa. Robin Drury was a friend of Paul Mann's who needed the money; they were making tapes for a book she hoped to sell. It seemed strange to employ a manager when she barely had a career, but Robin had talked her into it.

'Breakfast?' He passed her a boiled egg. 'Newspaper?' On page one was Hod Dibben's wife Mariella, who was now sleeping with the likes of President Kennedy (or so rumour had it.) She'd never taken a paper before, but now they were almost worth reading.

'I've found the name of a good solicitor ... Lucky has made an appeal. He says you lied on oath — to protect witnesses.'

She sighed. 'I promised Paula's friends I wouldn't mention them. And John's her brother — besides, I hit him too. It's not their fault that Lucky attacked me again. What can I do?'

'You must tell the police, or else you could be prosecuted. You've got to save your own skin, Christine. It's too late to help the others.'

'But I don't want to go to court again.'

'Stephen's trial is next month. The prosecution have asked you to testify.'

'And be labelled a prostitute?'

'People will see he's not a ponce. It's your chance to set the record straight — and anyway you don't have a choice. Let's finish the book and make a killing, and then you could leave the country.'

'What's the use? The newspaper hasn't paid me yet, and they changed my story. How do I know you won't do the same?'

'We could burn the tapes — or I could sell them to you for later. I won't be fobbed off though. I want fifteen thousand pounds.'

She made tea for herself and pottered around his flat, collecting the few possessions she'd kept since leaving Mandy's. She'd stay with Kim and Paula that night. She'd talk to her solicitor and get rid of Robin. She was better off alone.

~

Stephen sat nervously outside the courtroom with his solicitor. His hair was slicked back and he wore a morning suit. The crowd in the courtyard had shocked him, but he hoped that people would lose interest as the trial went on.

He laughed along as his solicitor cracked jokes, but he wasn't listening. He'd been in Brixton Prison for three weeks before a few friends bailed him out. Bill hadn't been in touch, but had sent on notice to leave Spring Cottage.

An exhibition of his sketches was opening soon. His portraits were his proudest achievements — they reminded him of the lives he'd lived and the many people he'd known. He wanted to be remembered by them.

Most of all, he had to protect his friends. Eugene was out of the picture, and Christine had turned against him. He didn't want to betray anyone else. Anyone could see that the charges against him were ridiculous, and he hoped that someone in the city could help him.

# CHAPTER 30

Christine's new manager, Walter Lyons, drove her to a block of government offices. She had stopped going out alone months before; she was public property, but didn't want to be. She was afraid Lucky might send his brothers after her.

The rumours surrounding her were mortifying — the newspaper stories where she was described as a call girl, a marriage-wrecker, and worse. She had tried to be truthful, but it seemed that she was to be punished for Jack Profumo's mistakes.

'I'm so pleased to meet you.' She eagerly extended her hand to Lord Denning. He led the Court of Appeal and was chosen by Harold Macmillan to investigate what was referred to as the Profumo Affair. He helped her into a chair. He was older than Stephen. His hair was white. She ran her fingers along the dusty edge of the oak desk.

'When did you meet Mr Profumo?'

'Two summers ago ... at Lord Astor's estate. I met Eugene there too.'

'How well do you know Ivanov?'

'We slept together once, after the party. It never happened again. He was friendly with Stephen.'

'And when did you next speak to Mr Profumo?'

'He took me out that week. Stephen encouraged me, so I agreed. I got to like him after a while.'

'Stephen ... Stephen Ward. Are you his girlfriend?'

'No — and I never have been. He's always taken an interest in me, though. We lived together for two years.'

Denning smiled to himself. It was Ward he wanted to know about. Ward was an embarrassment; he had to be stopped. The girl would not pose a problem, and the whole affair could be forgotten by September.

'Ward took you to an orgy in December 1961. Do you remember it?'

'I was there, but not for long. It's not my kind of thing. People having sex in groups ... they were all much older than me.'

'Was Ward enjoying himself?'

'He likes to watch. I think he stayed to the end when all the girls had gone, so that he could talk about politics with the other men.'

'Did you sleep with any of those men?' She shook her head. 'Did any of Ward's friends offer you money?'

'It was a private party.' She had a sinking feeling that Lord Denning was no different to the Fleet Street hacks who had butchered her story in print.

'Miss Rice-Davies tells me she accompanied you that night.'

'You've spoken to her already?'

'Just answer the question, Miss Keeler.' Lord Denning blew his nose.

'I shared a car with her — she was on her way to Peter's. But why are you talking to her? She doesn't know anything.'

He peered at Christine over the rim of his spectacles, with distaste. 'Miss Rice-Davies was most co-operative. I hope our interviews will be equally productive.' He took a photograph from a dossier. 'Do you recognise this man?'

'It's Mr Hollis — he used to come to our flat. He had some business with Stephen a couple of years ago.'

'Mr Hollis works for MI5. Did you understand the nature of his business?'

'Not really, I thought he was a spy for the government. He got Stephen and Eugene together; he telephoned Stephen a lot when I was with Jack. Stephen made me leave the room, but he always left the door open.'

She caught her breath, and continued. 'He asked me to find out secrets from Jack — about when the bombs were going to Germany. I refused. Then he made another phone-call ...'

Lord Denning shut the window and switched on a desk lamp. The room was dark and dusty. He clicked the tape recorder off.

'You're a very foolish girl, and you've made a lot of trouble for us,' he said slowly. 'All this nonsense about spies will do you no good. If you ever mention this again you will go to prison and I will make sure you never come out.'

# CHAPTER 31

Ronna Riccardo spoke in a scared whisper. After months of police harassment she was dragged to the docks of the Old Bailey. The building seemed huge, only a step away from prison.

'I — I've changed my statement,' she stammered. 'What I said about Dr Ward at the hearing — it isn't true.'

Mervyn Griffith-Jones, prosecuting counsel, boomed, 'Do you mean you lied?'

Ronna blushed, a shade pinker than her mohair sweater. 'Yes sir — and I regret it more than I can say.'

'Why did you lie? Don't you know perjury is a criminal offence?'

'The coppers made me do it, sir. They said they'd take my little sisters if I didn't squeal. My mother's dead and I work all hours for them.'

'And what is your profession?'

'Well, I'm a prostitute, of course!' A faint titter rose from the gallery.

'When did you meet Ward?'

Ronna chewed thoughtfully on a fingernail. 'About three years ago, at the Rose and Crown in Stepney. It's a pub, sir.'

'And you became friends?'

'Sort of. He was a punter for a while. Then he offered to help me out when I was in a spot of bother.'

'What sort of trouble was this?'

'I had a boyfriend — a GI, Silky Hawkins his name was. I wanted to spend time with him, when I wasn't working.'

Ronna looked over at the judge, Sir Archibald Marshall. He was reading his clerk's notes. 'Do continue,' he said brusquely.

'Doctor Ward liked me, and I reckoned he must have a nice gaff. So I asked him if I could take Silky there one day, and he agreed right away.' She smiled gratefully at Stephen, who seemed not to notice.

'So you entertained a man at the flat of the accused?' Mervyn Griffith-Jones swept before her. 'Did the man pay for sex?'

'No. I loved Silky you see — I let him have it for free.'

'Did Ward ask you for money?'

'Of course not!' Ronna was staggered by the idea. 'He was doing me a favour.'

Griffith-Jones was sceptical. 'The defendant invited you to a party on Lord Astor's estate. Why did you go?'

'I wanted to pick up some trade. I met lots of rich old gentlemen there, asking for a spanking; that's my speciality.'

'And did these gentlemen pay for your services?'

'Certainly. I made a lot of new contacts there. I earned enough for three weeks' rent.'

'Did you pass any of your earnings on to Ward?'

Ronna shook her head. 'Small beer to a man like the Doctor. I was just part of the scenery, really.'

'But in your last statement — '

'With respect, sir, I was under a lot of pressure. But I must tell you, no matter what I said before, Dr Ward never took no cash off me. He's been nothing but kind and I'd hate to see him in trouble on my account.'

~

'You lived with Ward, didn't you? Did he ask you to move in with him?' Griffith-Jones spat as he spoke, so that each point of fact became an accusation.

Mandy stroked her blue petalled hat and the tight gold curls that lay beneath. There on the witness stand, she felt that Judgment Day had arrived too soon.

'I met Stephen through Christine when we were working at Mr Murray's club. They took me in after a close friend died — I stayed for two months at the end of last year.'

'Did Ward ask you to pay rent?'

'I gave him money whenever I had it — towards the rent and some of the bills.'

'Did he force you to have sex with anyone?'

'No, never.' She raised her head and looked up to the gallery. It was important to her not to be branded as cheap; that would ruin her chances of pursuing her career, or making a good marriage.

Still, she felt sure she could turn Stephen's trial to her advantage. (The crowd had cheered as she stepped out of the taxi, and policemen dragged her away when a man in the crowd grabbed her coat.)

'Do you know Lord Astor?'

'Oh yes. We used to go to his house for weekends — there were some wonderful parties.'

'Have you slept with him?'

'Once, about two years ago.'

'Did he pay you for it?'

'Of course not!' She batted her eyelashes in the jury's direction.

Griffith-Jones frowned. 'Where did you meet Dr Savundra?' he asked, taking Mandy by surprise. She hadn't thought about Emil, or heard his name, in months.

'At Stephen's flat — while I was staying there.'

'Did you have sex with Doctor Savundra?'

'Yes — a few times.' Griffith-Jones nodded, and she knew she had dropped herself in it.

'Where did this happen?'

'In Stephen's flat — in the spare bedroom.'

'And where was Ward at this time?'

'I don't know — probably in the living room, or maybe the kitchen.' Griffith-Jones turned away from her with a grimace, clearly disgusted by her and Ward.

'Did Savundra give you money? What did you do with it?'

'He was generous,' she sighed. 'He gave me fifteen or twenty pounds.'

'Did you give this money to Ward?'

'Absolutely not.'

'But it went towards the rent, I suppose?'

Mandy said nothing. Her head ached, she felt terrible. It had seemed so glamorous this morning when she and Christine were sitting in Vidal Sassoon's, getting their hair set for the juiciest trial in years. Now she felt small and shallow, yet she could still be Stephen's undoing.

~

Christine looked out as Mr Lyons' car approached the Old Bailey. Someone screamed her name and the crowd drew closer. An egg hit the window; the sound was loud as gunfire.

She got out of the car in the judges' private car park and the driver took her through the courts' back door. She sat with the other witnesses, the whores and their tricks. One was a witness for the prosecution who mumbled her name, Vickie.

A clerk brought her a glass of water and she slipped down two tranquillisers. She went to the toilet and checked herself in the mirror, alone for a second. Then she was called to the courtroom, up to the witness box.

The questions began and she answered in a monotone. She saw Stephen conferring with his barrister, and was shocked by how thin he looked.

No one really believed he was a ponce; he wasn't even that interested in sex. He'd used Christine, and all his other girls to win influence with men of power, but lately he had lost his grip.

'Have you ever had sex for money?'

'Never ...'

Griffith-Jones scuttled towards her, knees bent, clasping his hands together. 'But we have already heard the testimony of Major James Eynon, who told us that he paid you for sex about six times in the home of the accused.'

'I've known Major Jim since the Cabaret Club and he's my friend, not Stephen's. I didn't mention him to Stephen because I wanted to protect his privacy — he's married, you see.'

'You claimed in your statement that Ward introduced you to a man who would give you money. Was this man not his friend, the financier Charles Clore?'

'No! ... I mean, I don't know. I only met him once, for dinner with Stephen. I didn't sleep with him and he didn't offer me money; we haven't seen each other since and I don't remember his last name.'

'Were you offered money by any other men?'

'Yes — Jack Profumo wanted to buy me a flat near the Houses of Parliament, while I was living with Stephen — I didn't take it very seriously though. He once gave me twenty pounds for my mother, and a lighter with my name engraved on it.'

'I have no further questions to ask of Miss Keeler.'

She sighed, facing the piggy little prosecuting barrister head on. Stephen's barrister stood up, glancing briefly at his list of prepared questions.

# CHAPTER 32

Stephen's trial was now eight days old. He was not sleeping and ate little, relying on pills to get by. Noel, the son of a friend, had put him up. Christine had a crush on Noel once, but Stephen had discouraged it. He regretted that now.

He looked up at Mandy and Christine, who sat close together in the public gallery. Mandy nodded at him, but Christine flinched.

The prosecution called for Vickie Barrett, a tart he had paid for a few months ago. She wasn't pretty; she looked cheap, and her cheapness reflected on him. He guessed the police had grilled her and ground her down, until she said what they wanted to hear.

'He picked me up on Oxford Street,' she said. 'He said there was a man at his flat who wanted a girl. He drove me there. He showed me the bedroom door — he told me the man was waiting there.'

Stephen stood up. 'I must protest, your honour — she's lying!' James Burge shook his head, touching Stephen's arm. He sat down again.

'There were four men in the bedroom. One of them picked up a horsewhip and asked me to beat him. The others joined in — they paid me a pound for each stroke.'

'Do you recognise her?' Mandy whispered to Christine, wide-eyed. Christine shook her head. The questions continued.

'When we finished, Mr Ward collected the money. He said he'd look after it, and if I came again he'd save up and find me a flat.'

'This is a pack of lies from start to end!' said Stephen. 'I barely know the girl. I only slept with her once, and no one else was there.'

~

His solicitor addressed the court. 'There are two questions before us today: are these young women prostitutes, and if they are, has the defendant been living off their immoral earnings? Let us consider first of all the girls.

'Miss Barrett and Miss Riccardo are both known prostitutes. The defendant does not deny having paid for their services on occasion, and Miss

Riccardo even thought of him as a friend. However, there is no evidence to suggest that the witnesses have been soliciting clients on his behalf. Parts of Miss Riccardo's original testimony have been retracted; and I suspect that Miss Barrett's statements are equally unreliable. One cannot underestimate the pressure that witnesses have been put under given the controversial nature of this case.

'As for Miss Keeler and Miss Rice-Davies, they are not hardened prostitutes; they are teenagers who have made mistakes and fallen prey to the temptations of easy money. I do not believe that they are any less moral than other young people struggling to make lives for themselves in London today.

'The defendant was a father figure to these girls and, far from luring them into degradation, encouraged them to better themselves. He has, like many professional men, paid for sex — and he admits that he loves the company of women. He is a respected professional with no need to depend on anyone else for money or status. It is his misfortune to have been linked with scandal, but he must not be allowed to take the blame for the misdoings of others.

'Ignore the tabloid headlines which do not inform but merely titillate; recognise the evidence brought by the prosecution as a tissue of lies. Consider the character of the defendant and his excellent reputation until now, and I am sure you will find him to be not guilty.'

# CHAPTER 33

Court adjourned, and Stephen left the Old Bailey. He put on dark glasses to protect himself from the eyes of the crowd. He walked through the gates, smiled for the press and, without answering questions, pushed towards his car, where a friend, Julie, waited. They drove off quickly.

They arrived at Noel's flat in Chelsea about fifteen minutes later. Stephen sat down at Noel's desk. He began writing letters, addressing and sealing envelopes. Then he called his friend Tom, an *Express* reporter, and asked him to come to the flat. He arrived within half an hour.

'I've been talking to Ronna Riccardo,' Tom said. 'She has told me, on the record, that the police have been fixing the evidence. We can prove your innocence ...'

'To whom — your readers? I'll be in prison tomorrow, Griffith-Jones and Marshall have cooked it up together.' Julie passed him a glass of brandy and he raised it to his lips.

'But you can appeal ...?' Julie asked nervously.

'Christine and Mandy's evidence is enough to get me put away. Marshall will go for the maximum sentence — maybe seven years. And what then? I have too many enemies — men who could have me killed.' He thought about the documents that had been stolen by that barmaid, Wendy. She didn't work at the pub anymore.

Julie topped up their glasses. She was only twenty-three, a lovely singer from a coffee bar in Soho. It would be better if she forgot him. He reached for the letters he had written and handed them to Tom.

Tom thumbed through the envelopes, all stamped. 'They're suicide notes, aren't they? I won't be a part of this.'

'Fine.' Stephen's cigarette burned out; Julie fetched him another. 'Keep yours, but don't read it until the verdict's out.'

~

The photographer drove to Bryanston Mews. A month ago it had been swarming with press, but Ward hadn't stayed there since his arrest. The photographer was covering the Profumo affair for the *Express*, and had been called out to meet Ward at his request.

Inside the flat it was chilly and damp, abandoned and unloved. Soft, rotten fruit was shrivelling in a glass bowl, and a weeks-old *Radio Times* flopped over the television set. A young man, tall, good-looking, and wearing a black cape over a tuxedo, had opened the door to the photographer. He sat silently on an armchair, sipping glasses of red wine. Stephen was at his desk.

'Come over here, please — I want you to get a picture of this.' The photographer snapped around him as he wrote to Henry Brooke, the Home Secretary. 'Can you develop these tonight? I need them for tomorrow morning. You must bring them to me first thing — I'm taking this letter to the Home Office before I go to court, and I want to keep some proof for when the verdict's announced.'

'It's nearly half past eleven, Stephen.' The young man walked to the door. 'I really must be going ... I have a dinner date.'

'Very well, I'm just about done here. I'm picking Julie up in Chelsea and driving her home, and then I'll go for a spin somewhere.' His fingers trembled as he buttoned his overcoat. He turned off the lights and the three men drove away separately.

The photographer returned to the *Express* offices and went straight into the darkroom.

~

Noel Howard-Jones returned from a late supper with his fiancée, and went straight to bed. As he lay alone in the darkness, he heard the footsteps in the hallway.

'That must be Stephen,' he thought, and fell asleep.

He woke at eight thirty, put on a dressing gown and knocked on the door to the study, where the telephone was ringing. Stephen lay inert on the sofa: his skin was tinged dark purple, his mouth hung open and there was a red mark on his chin.

The telephone stopped ringing. Noel slapped his face; Stephen breathed once, and then stopped again. Noel called for an ambulance. The press gathered outside as Stephen was carried to hospital on a stretcher.

Noel remained in his study. Jars of sedatives were strewn across the carpet, and the bottle of whiskey they had opened was among the mess. He reached for the envelope addressed to him in Stephen's own handwriting. The doorbell rang, and he put the letter aside.

The photographer who Stephen had met the previous night was at the door. He shook Noel's hand.

'Mr Ward asked me to call ... I can take him to the office now, if he's ready.'

'I'm sorry. He took an overdose last night ...'

'Oh, no.' The photographer went pale.

'I can't understand it ... I thought he was going to fight this.' Noel went back inside, trying to remember where he had put the letter. 'Where did he get to last night? What happened to him?'

The photographer hurried back to his Morris Minor and drove quickly to work. He ran into the darkroom, where he had left the prints to dry. They were gone, and the negatives were nowhere to be seen.

# EPILOGUE
## 1967

*It was a warm, cloudy morning in July. On a folding bed in Mr Lyons' rented office, part of an old warehouse in Bow, I lay awake as hours ticked by. Newspaper clippings surrounded me, gathering dust. At ten to seven he let himself in.*

*'Brace yourself for some terrible news, my dear.' He placed a mug of coffee by the bed. I turned on my side and tied back my hair with a stray rubber band. 'It's Stephen ... he's dying.'*

*'What happened?' Our eyes met over the* Telegraph.

*'He took an overdose last night. He's in hospital now, but nothing can be done for him.'*

*I felt as if I'd been punched; my stomach churned, and I was suddenly out of breath.*

*'Can you please open the window?' I gasped. Mr Lyons did so and went into the kitchenette, cut bread and put it under the grill. I lifted the mug to my lips and threw the coffee down.*

*I stood up and tied my dressing gown. I went to the window and picked up the jar of Nembutal that I'd left on the sill. I looked out of the window; cars and people crawled like ants, thirty feet below.*

*I brushed my teeth at the sink, and spread marmalade on two wedges of toast. Later that day, Stephen was found guilty of living off the immoral earnings of Mandy and I. It took him three more days to die.*

~

*The walls of my new house in Linhope Street, Marylebone, were bare. Paula and I sat on the mattress, the only piece of furniture I had, drinking white wine out of paper cups. I bought the house with the £13,000 I had finally earned from the* Express.

*I sold my story again to the* Sunday Herald, *hoping that this version would be closer to the truth. I earned a further £7,000, and bought a bungalow for mum and my stepdad in Wokingham, near Wraysbury.*

*Within days of moving in, I was arrested. The police had found the tapes I'd made with Robin Drury for the book I wanted to write. They heard me talking about Lucky Gordon and how I'd agreed to keep Fenton and Commachio, the two witnesses to his attack on me,* out of the court case. And Paula's brother, John, had confessed as well. So I was charged with committing perjury at Lucky's trial, and had to take out a loan to cover my legal fees.

'The prosecution want to make a deal,' Mr Lyons told me. 'If you admit perjury, the other charge —wrongfully accusing Lucky of assault — will be dropped, and you'll get a shorter sentence.'

I pleaded guilty, and was jailed for nine months, while Lucky walked free.

~

I waited for my father in the visitors' room at Holloway Prison. I'd said goodbye to him when I was four years old, waving from our air raid shelter. I knew very little about him, though I often wondered what kind of man he might be.

He contacted Mr Lyons during my perjury trial, and we hit it off instantly; he sat in the police box, close to me, smiling and making me brave.

A few husbands and boyfriends came in; children and grandparents followed, and dad was at the back. 'Christine!' he said, grasping my hands tightly. His fingers were long and slim.

'How are you bearing up, girl?'

'I'm coping, dad — keeping my head down.' Prison life was hard, but I found the routine almost reassuring. My cellmate, Libby, was a good sort.

'How's your mum?' he asked.

'Missing me, I think.' I hadn't told her about dad yet. I knew she hated him for leaving us when he did.

'Be good to her, Christine. I'm sorry things didn't work out for us three.' His eyes brimmed with tears whenever he talked about the life he'd led without mum and me; his long nose, his full mouth were the double of mine.

I also wondered how different my life might have been if he'd stayed. I might never have run away to London.

'You haven't changed a bit, you know. You've still got that gap between your two front teeth — '

I shook my head and he stopped mid-sentence.

'Please don't say that, dad. Everything's changed, you know that.'

He touched my forehead. 'You're a good, honest kid, Chrissie.'

I smiled weakly. The warden called time and we said our goodbyes. I went back to my cell and smoked the cigarettes he'd brought along.

A postcard came from Mandy. She was in Holland, singing and dancing in a club. She never did have much of a voice, but maybe all those music lessons Peter paid for had been worth it after all.

I had dozens of letters from men I'd never met, some threatening or obscene. One was a marriage proposal. While reading, I began to wonder what life would be like for me when I got out.

~

London was changing, quicker than I could keep up with it, when I was released from Holloway Prison after serving six months. Harold Macmillan had resigned, and a new

Labour government was in power under Harold Wilson. I returned to my empty house, inviting dad, who was out of work, to stay.

All-night clubs were opening all over London, now owned by the Kray Twins who I'd known since I was with Peter. They were now more famous than me; we met at one of their clubs in Mayfair, and were photographed together.

At the time of Jack's resignation I believed my modelling career was over. But there was work to be had, if I was prepared to trade on my name.

Mr Lyons sold the rights to my story all over Europe. The profits went directly to Millwarren, his company. He gave me money to buy things but kept the larger share. I had no control over what was written about me, so I agreed to whatever he suggested, and tried not to care.

Dad got a job at one of Billy Butlin's holiday camps in Clacton, Essex. I told mum about him and invited her down. She wouldn't set foot in my house until I asked him to go. I never saw him again.

As I furnished my new house, I remembered how exciting it had been to come to live in London when I was just a teenager, and how my life had changed after I met Stephen.

The house on Linhope Street was big and lonely; I found it hard to settle there. I sold it after two years and went to stay with my mother in Wokingham. It was quiet and after being talked about for so long, I wanted a bit of peace.

I often drove out to Wraysbury, to see my old schoolfriend Jackie White. She had broken up with a man and persuaded me to meet him.

He was Jim Levermore, a civil engineer, six feet tall with green eyes and curly brown hair. Unlike the men I'd known in London, he didn't talk much.

'It doesn't matter to you — who I am?' I asked him over a glass of sherry at the Golden Fleece. 'All the stories in the papers?'

He just laughed, and kissed me. Eventually he said, 'Will you marry me?'

I thought he'd never ask. It was a long shot but of course I said yes.

It happened very quickly. I bought a bungalow a few streets away from my mother. I had my hair cut into a jaw-length bob with a long fringe. We were married at the district registrar's in Reading, by special license and without publicity.

Shortly after the wedding, Jim went to work in Germany. I stayed at home. I was pregnant; our son was born in 1966. His name was James, like the one I lost, but mum called him Jimmy.

~

At night, after I'd put the baby to bed, I'd soak for an hour in a deep, hot bath, reading paperbacks and listening to the radio. I got out after the Nine O'Clock News and wandered into my bedroom, wrapped in a towel. The window was open and the curtains blew, revealing a man outside, staring at me.

I walked back to the hall and dialled the police. They came with tracker dogs but the man had gone. Days later I came back from the grocers' with Jimmy to find the bathroom window smashed and the back door hanging open. Nothing was taken but my wardrobe had been ransacked, and underwear was scattered across the bedroom floor.

*Mr Lyons came as soon as he heard, bringing a dog for me. 'You're going to need some protection, my dear. Now, I must show you this before you hear it from someone else.'*

*He took a well-thumbed magazine from his briefcase and turned to the middle page. The blurb was in German, but I recognised the man in the picture; it was my husband, Jim, in the arms of another woman, beside a smaller photograph of me.*

*'You've got yourself in a mess again,' said Mr Lyons, passing me a handkerchief to sob on. 'There's still the sum of your debts to repay: you can't hide from the world forever, not when there are so many exciting opportunities for a girl like you.'*

*I went back to London, renting a flat in Weymouth Street. Jimmy stayed in Wokingham with mum at first, until I got myself settled. I was divorcing Jim on the grounds of desertion, and the legal fees were more than I could afford — so I quickly accepted an offer to pose topless for a new fashion magazine.*

*Driving up to London, with Jimmy in the back of my Austin Martin and the dog with me in front, I watched the countryside flash by. The hill where I grew up and the forest behind it were just specks in the distance, the caravan I'd lived in probably a heap of wrecked metal by then. I didn't slow down until we reached London.*

*How trapped I'd felt in Wraysbury, and how easily I'd escaped; but there was no turning back this time, however much I wanted to. I'd lost the only place I ever called a home, and there was nowhere left to run to but the city.*

# AFTERWORD

'It's not really *about* sex, is it?'

That was a friend's first reaction after reading an early draft of *Wicked Baby*. My first novel — I call it a novella — planted itself in 1989, when I saw *Scandal*, a film about the Profumo Affair, at the Ilford Odeon. The notion of being a 'good-time girl' appealed, but more for the freedom and independence than anything else.

Seven years later, after I'd been to university and moved to Brighton, I found three books about the Profumo Affair in a second-hand bookshop. By then I was a writer — in my head, anyway — and after reading for a few days, I found there was a story I wanted to tell. A fascination with how events unfolded, and sympathy for Christine Keeler. It's a coming-of-age novel, a tale of seduction and betrayal.

*Wicked Baby* took shape over the next five years, during which time I met and married my husband, and gave birth to my eldest child, and drifted between North and South (settling, for a while, in the Midlands.) I continued to research the scandal, with limited resources — at first, not even the price of a trip to Cliveden. This only made me more determined. If I had written it later, it would probably be longer. But it wouldn't have the raw, staccato quality that made it mine.

Much of *Wicked Baby* was written by hand on scrap notes, then copied onto an electronic typewriter that my mother had acquired from the school where she worked. I finally bought a word processor in a charity shop, which although laughably primitive now, helped me enormously then. To have written a novel by my thirtieth birthday felt like a victory, even if it wouldn't get published for a few more years.

Like many first-time authors, I experienced rejection. So I moved onto another project, leaving my manuscript in the drawer. Then in 2004 — a year after my second child was born — I decided to self-publish. Vanity or otherwise, I slowly gained a small but supportive readership.

Nine years later, I was back in Brighton. My second novel, *The Mmm Girl*, had been published by a small press, and I was busily working on multiple projects. The fiftieth anniversary of the Profumo Affair inspired me to write several articles, and to think once again about *Wicked Baby*.

The book's compactness made it ripe for digital reading, I thought. Early on I resolved to make only a few revisions. The non-fiction pieces I selected to accompany it — two of which are previously unpublished — focus on how the scandal has been represented in popular culture, and its impact on society.

Half a century has passed, and the establishment still stands, in slightly different form: political lobbying, media corruption, and inequality are all rife. Celebrity culture as we know it began on the day a young man fired his gun at the window of a quiet mews house in London, and two women were thrown into the spotlight.

*Tara Hanks, August 2014*

# NIGHTWAVES: THE EARLY 1960s

*"Sexual intercourse began*
*In nineteen sixty-three*
*(which was rather late for me) —*
*Between the end of the Chatterley ban*
*And the Beatles' first LP".*

So begins Philip Larkin's 'Annus Mirabilis,' read aloud by the dour English poet. That defining moment was epitomised by the Profumo Affair, which made headlines in the spring of 1963. Larkin's recording is one of several soundbites, overlapping each other as a prelude to 'The Early 1960s,' a special edition of BBC Radio 3's weekly arts programme, *Nightwaves*, marking a half-century since this 'annus mirabilis,' and broadcast in December 2013 to coincide with the opening of Andrew Lloyd-Webber's stage musical, *Stephen Ward*.

'There's undoubtedly a magnetism about the girl, an electricity when she enters,' a male observer said of Christine Keeler, focusing on her 'knee-length black leather boots, with tall, clicking Spanish heels.' This fetishistic image is undercut with another man's voice, speaking about Profumo. 'He lied and lied and lied: lied to his friends; lied to his family; lied to the House of Commons.' But this note of outrage is quickly subsumed as we return to the smitten male. 'Watch the head turn to flick the hair into place,' he drools, 'and the tongue surreptitiously moisten the lipstick ... '

With the opening bars to The Beatles' first single, 'Please Please Me,' in the background, presenter Matthew Sweet introduces his guests. Lynda Baron, best-known for her role as Nurse Gladys Emmanuel in the sitcom, *Open All Hours*, began her television career in 1962, appearing in an episode of *The Rag Trade*. For her, 1963 was 'a watershed year, though one didn't realise that at the time.'

Feminist writer Bea Campbell was sixteen in 1963. She recalls that D.H. Lawrence's infamous novel, *Lady Chatterley's Lover*, was being passed around by pupils at the single-sex Carlisle County High, 'leaving girls perplexed.' That book was still banned in Australia, where Sir Geoffrey Robertson — now a Q.C. — recalled hearing playground rhymes about the Profumo Affair: 'Mandy Rice, Mandy Rice, twice as nice at half the price.'

*Stephen Ward: The Musical* begins with a tableau of Ward's waxwork, as it stood in Madame Tussaud's of Blackpool during the 1960s — between Adolf Hitler and John George Hague, the 'acid bath murderer.' Don Black remarks that he did not write with the aim of 'exonerating' Ward — but the disgraced osteopath hardly deserved to be in such grisly company.

Robertson's polemical *Stephen Ward Was Innocent, OK?* was inspired by a conversation with Andrew Lloyd-Webber in September 2013, at the funeral of David Frost. Arguing that 'there was no crime ... they [Keeler, Rice-Davies *et al*] were not prostitutes,' he condemns Ward's conviction for living off immoral earnings as 'injustice within the law.'

Richard Davenport-Hines, author of *An English Affair* (2013), echoes Robertson's view: 'A man was identified and a crime was fixed on him.' He also notes 'shocking and scandalous pressure on witnesses ... terrorisation and coercion of very vulnerable women.'

Recalling the famous story of Keeler's first meeting with Profumo — while skinny-dipping at Cliveden, Lord Astor's estate — Lynda Baron admits, 'the swimming pool loomed large in the grey London of that time,' noting that 'those who had money and position did not appear at the trial.'

Bea Campbell praises Robertson's book as the first to focus on 'issue of process' in the case. However, she counters that while Stephen Ward may not have been guilty of any crime, he and his powerful friends were 'a disgrace.'

Keeler, as Campbell points out, had 'a rotten life,' escaping a deprived, abusive background, only to be 'encircled by violent, predatory men.' Christine trusted Ward because he didn't want sex with her, but — despite their Pygmalion-like relationship — Campbell believes Keeler was used by upper class men who traded in pretty young girls. 'She had no judgment,' Campbell says, and was 'ruined by men.'

Describing Keeler as a 'good-time girl,' Baron responds that while her judgment may have been flawed, she still had choices: 'You could always go and work in Woolworth's.' Richard Davenport-Hines alludes to the happier fate of Keeler's friend. 'Mandy was more resilient,' he states. 'She made her own sexual choices.' Both women, however, have endured 'a continuing process of rubbishing and humiliating by right-wing, misogynist newspapers.'

Campbell criticises the 'enterprise to rehabilitate Stephen Ward,' speculating that he was 'at the centre of a racket — dirty business — was it a spy scandal or a sex scandal? Girls traded — Cold War, power and state — the state franchised out their dirty work to Ward, and lost control of the story.'

Robertson dismisses this as merely a 'conspiracy theory,' describing Ward as 'an innocent man — whether he was a good man or a bad man is another matter.' The scandal, says Robertson, was a 'leering, lecherous product of an utterly censorious time,' adding that a Tory M.P. caught in a sex club today would be thrown out of Parliament.

But although indiscretions can destroy a political career, corruption is not a thing of the past. Journalist Andy Coulson was recently convicted for phone-hacking. A former editor of the now-defunct *News of the World*, Coulson was already under suspicion when Prime Minister David Cameron appointed him as his Director of Communications.

Sex didn't really begin in 1963, although it may have seemed that way. Richard Davenport-Hines offers an historian's perspective: 'Britain's sexual attitudes had been changing since 1945.' And the contraceptive pill — approved by the National Health Service in 1962 — 'gave women the freedom to choose,' says Lynda Baron.

And before the Profumo Affair, there was the *Chatterley* trial. Jeremy Hutchinson Q.C., who defended both cases, believes that Ward's prosecution was 'a revenge match.' Hutchinson represented Keeler, who he says, despite a 'hard look in her eyes,' was far from the 'wicked prostitute' of tabloid legend. As for Ward, 'he was set up…they were out to get him.' Lord Hutchinson echoes Geoffrey Robertson when he describes the case as 'the one great remaining miscarriage of justice' and 'the last fling of the establishment.'

Lynda Baron remarks that the *Chatterley* trial exposed 'men's fear that women would learn more about sex … and expect them to up their game.' And in the wake of the Profumo Affair, comments Bea Campbell, 'the dead hand of respectability in the Labour Party' incited a Puritanical crusade against the Tories, who were then rather more liberal towards abortion.

'As an advocate in the criminal courts of the Fifties, Sixties and Seventies,' Hutchinson recalls, 'I had the luck to practice in the period when we were dismantling the power of the establishment.' He cites the legalisation of homosexuality; the abolition of capital punishment; and an attack on 'the culture of secrecy which was so paramount at the time.'

But what was 'the establishment,' and does it still exist? 'We still have a secret state that tells us it has our best interests at heart,' Matthew Sweet concludes. 'And perhaps we still don't quite know how to talk about sex. Where do we stand now?'

# KISS AND TELL: FIFTY YEARS OF SCANDAL

*"In my day, there was a sense of style about the whole thing, you know. Christine Keeler, Mandy Rice-Davies ... Gorgeous little women who kept their mouths shut and just looked gorgeous, and gave the whole thing an air of dignity."* – Patsy Stone, *Absolutely Fabulous*

Patsy was half-right. They *were* gorgeous — but they didn't keep their mouths shut. In 1963, Tory cabinet minister John Profumo was forced to resign after his affair with a young model, Christine Keeler, made headlines.

Carol Dyhouse, a cultural historian and professor of gender studies, has considered the impact of the Profumo Affair, and its links to the sexual revolution, in her latest book, *Girl Trouble*. While acknowledging that both girls were denounced as 'shameless tarts' — by the same newspapers that spurred their notoriety — she argues that 'both were capable of standing up for themselves, and refused to be silenced.'

Fifty years on, the Profumo Affair is still news — though the story has largely been told by men. Richard Davenport-Hines's *An English Affair* is the latest study of a sex scandal which, it's sometimes said, marked the end of an 'age of deference' and heralded the dawning of the tabloid culture that still prevails today (despite Lord Leveson's best efforts.)

Profumo wasn't the only victim, however. Keeler's former friend, Dr Stephen Ward, became the scapegoat when he was falsely charged with living off the immoral earnings of various young women, including Mandy Rice-Davies. Reporting on Ward's trial, Rebecca West noted that Christine possessed 'a terrified dignity,' while Sybille Bedford saw only 'a blank absence of spirit.' Both women, however, were struck by Keeler's dark beauty, captured in an iconic nude portrait by photographer Lewis Morley.

'In the early Sixties there were girls you touched and girls you didn't, and the girls who could be touched were, and all the time,' Tanya Gold wrote in

*The Telegraph* in 2012. 'Keeler was too early for robust feminism, and when the story broke she went down ... '

Ward committed suicide, while Christine was convicted of perjury and packed off to Holloway Prison. By 1964, Harold Macmillan's government had collapsed; and Mandy Rice-Davies published a memoir, *The Mandy Report*, its title a cheeky riposte to Lord Denning's report. It's often said that Mandy is the 'true survivor' of the debacle. In 1980, she wrote her autobiography, *Mandy*. A lover of romantic fiction, she has also penned two novels: *Today and Tomorrow*, and *The Scarlet Thread*.

In 1967, Christine Keeler sold her story to the *News of the World*, which had newly been acquired by Rupert Murdoch. Her full-length memoir, *Nothing But ...* , was published in 1983. An updated version was released to tie in with the 1989 film, *Scandal*.

Unhappy with the results, Keeler penned a third book, *The Truth at Last*, in 2001. It was reissued in 2012, under the title *Secrets and Lies*. Sensationally, Keeler has claimed that Ward was a Soviet spy — and the rumour persists, though the available evidence is sketchy. 'Her wish to retrieve her past is understandable,' novelist Jenny Diski wrote in the *London Review of Books*. 'Much better for the *amour propre* to have been Mata Hari than a party girl ... '

'We have much to thank Christine Keeler for,' Diski admitted. 'The rumours at the time were delightful, confirming everything we'd always suspected about the sanctimonious, repressive establishment. Let's remember the foolishness and arrogance of the privileged ... '

In recent years, both women have participated in further dramatisations of their lives. *Keeler*, a stage play written by Gill Adams, is touring the UK, while Mandy Rice-Davies is a consultant on Andrew Lloyd-Webber's musical, *Stephen Ward*. Earlier this year, she narrated a BBC radio play by Charlotte Williams. The title, *Well He Would, Wouldn't He?*, refers to Mandy's famous retort at Ward's trial, now immortalised in the *Oxford Dictionary of Quotations*.

Profumo's wife, Valerie Hobson, is remembered in *Bringing the House Down*, written by her son, David Profumo; while Bronwen Astor, whose husband was also caught up in the scandal, is the subject of a 2001 biography.

Sex scandals continue to titillate, at home and abroad — exposing men as diverse as Italian premier Silvio Berlusconi, and Wikileaks founder Julian Assange, and bold, vocal (and vilified) women, like White House intern Monica Lewinsky, and double-agent Anna Chapman. Beneath the superficial veneer of gossip, the ugly realities of prostitution, racism, homophobia, sexual harassment and rape are all too often ignored.

However, perhaps due to the outspokenness of the women involved, or simply because it happened first, the Profumo Affair has remained a blueprint for scandal — and held its place in the public consciousness for half a century.

*This article was first published at ForBooksSake.net on July 10th, 2013*

# 'WELL HE WOULD, WOULDN'T HE?'

*Well He Would, Wouldn't He?* is a radio play by Charlotte Williams (pseudonym of Sussex-born author and musician Charlotte Greig.) It marks the fiftieth anniversary of the Profumo Affair, retold by one of its chief protagonists: Mandy Rice-Davies.

In 1963, Mandy was 18: a model, showgirl and socialite. Originally from a middle-class family in Solihull, she had come to London to seek her fortune, and found herself implicated in one of the most infamous trials of the twentieth century.

The titular quote refers to Mandy's response, when told in court that Lord Astor had denied sleeping with her: '*Well, he would say that, wouldn't he?*' That retort has since been published in the Oxford Dictionary of Quotations. Sir Ivan Lawrence, a junior counsel at the time, recently claimed that Davies never actually said this. She replied in a letter to *The Times*, 'The palest ink is not always better than the best of memory, Sir Ivan — besides, I have before me the court transcript.'

The play is narrated by Davies herself, with Aimee-Ffion Edwards (best-known for her role as 'Sketch' in TV's *Skins*) playing the younger Mandy. The action is punctuated by music from the era, from bubblegum pop to Bob Dylan and Nina Simone.

Davies describes herself at the time as 'a hapless teenager,' and is depicted as a wide-eyed *ingénue*. Nonetheless, she was nobody's fool, as shown in the scene when she persuades Bill Astor and Dr Stephen Ward to pay for a housewarming party.

With tongue firmly in cheek, Mandy would later declare herself 'another Lady Hamilton.' Her illustrious conquests included the Earl of Dudley, Douglas Fairbanks Jr, and George Hamilton. Her slightly older friend,

Christine Keeler, introduced her to some of Ward's high-ranking friends, including Soviet diplomat Eugene Ivanov. It was Keeler's tangled affairs — with both Ivanov and Tory minister John Profumo — that would trigger a major political scandal.

Mandy later became the girlfriend of notorious 'slum landlord' Peter Rachman. In contrast to his thuggish reputation, Davies describes Rachman as 'educated and intelligent.' Devastated by his death in November 1962, she attempted suicide. While recovering, Mandy moved into Ward's flat. In December, Christine's aggrieved boyfriend, Johnny Edgecombe, fired shots at the building, and the incident made headlines.

'As it turned out, the press knew far more than the government did,' Davies reflects. 'They went on the rampage.' Shortly after Profumo's resignation, Mandy was arrested at Heathrow Airport, and detained at Holloway Prison for eight days on a charge of driving without a valid licence.

While in jail, she was questioned about her friendship with Ward by Chief Inspector Samuel Herbert. 'Although I felt certain that nothing I could say could damage Stephen,' she admits, 'I had the feeling that I was being dealt an arranged set of cards.'

A month later, Mandy was charged with stealing a television set. 'It was now clear,' she says, 'that the charge was being held over me until I agreed to give evidence against Stephen.'

In June 1963, Ward was arrested and charged with living off immoral earnings over a period of two years. His trial began on July 22$^{nd}$, and Mandy was called to the witness stand. Of the prosecuting attorney, Mervyn Griffith-Jones, Mandy recalls, 'his whole demeanour implied moral disapproval.' She described his closing speech as 'a public flogging.'

'Stephen was being tried for his lifestyle, not for any crime he'd committed,' she argues. 'He was an oddball; his principles were a bit wavery, but he didn't exploit anyone … and he certainly never asked me directly to sleep with anyone.' To the court, she insisted that 'He hasn't done anything wrong. You might as well arrest every bachelor in London!'

Despite claims that Ward was involved in a spy ring, Davies considers him politically naïve. 'Unseen forces within the establishment needed a scapegoat,' she says darkly. 'Someone to blame for the mess.'

'Griffith-Jones was trying to make me out to be a prostitute, which I certainly wasn't,' she claims.

Ward's well-to-do chums were noticeably absent in his hour of need. 'Stephen didn't want Bill Astor and his friends to testify,' Mandy explains. 'He didn't think he would need them to, and anyway, he didn't want to put them in the public spotlight. By the time he realised that he needed help, it was too late.'

On July 31$^{st}$, Ward was found unconscious in his flat, having taken an overdose of sleeping tablets. He died three days later, after being convicted *in absentia*. 'I was truly shocked and felt personal guilt,' Mandy admits. 'Christine was stricken with grief. We stayed away from his funeral. We were all responsible, in a way.'

'Ward's girls were plainly not prostitutes,' Lord Goodman said later. 'It was an historic injustice which took place in full view of everybody, clear to the world at large.'

*Well He Would, Wouldn't He?* depicts the era — and Mandy's part in it — evocatively, combining her memories with evidence from Ward's trial. Her youth and quick wit are apparent, but her tough survivor's instinct is somewhat downplayed.

During the 1960s, Davies managed a chain of restaurants. She went on to become a singer, actress and novelist, and now lives quietly with her husband of twenty-five years. In her own autobiography, Keeler wrote, 'I feel she's still the same old Mandy, telling people what they want to hear.'

'I think that because I was so young, I was able to recover,' Mandy concludes. 'I could have dressed in sackcloth and sprinkled myself with ashes, but what I did was to take a long, hard look at myself ... I hope that never again will anyone be able to point the finger at me and say, *Come this way, please.*'

*This article was originally published at TaraHanks.com on March 1st, 2013*

# RUMOURS

Lord Denning's report on the Profumo Affair was published fifty years this week. Though dismissed as a government whitewash, its steamy topic made this official enquiry an unlikely bestseller. At the same time, a very different version was unfolding in the pages of a new satirical magazine, *Private Eye*. This is the subject of Colin Shindler's radio play, *Rumours*.

Christopher Booker, then 26, was the magazine's editor, assisted by Richard Ingrams and Willie Rushton. All three had attended the same private school, though Rushton was in national service when the others studied at Oxford and Cambridge.

The play begins — and ends — with a lawsuit. The first, filed by Randolph Churchill, involved writs being issued among all thirteen staff. Booker was preoccupied with his other job, as political scriptwriter for ITV's *That Was the Week That Was*. Rushton often appeared on the show, impersonating Harold Macmillan (there is a running joke that viewers believed he was actually Prime Minister.)

The affairs of a 21 year-old model, Christine Keeler, were first publicised in December 1962, when an angry ex-lover, Johnny Edgecombe, fired shots outside the London flat she shared with Dr Stephen Ward. But gossips claimed that she had also been the lover of powerful men, including the Soviet naval attaché, Eugene Ivanov.

In early 1963, this story was parodied in *Private Eye* — with Keeler named only as 'Miss Gay Fun-Loving.' As the play reveals, 'Everyone knows that *Private Eye* prints rumours — that's why people buy it.'

Ingrams was initially sceptical of another rumour — that Keeler had been involved with John Profumo, the Minister for War, while at the same time seeing Ivanov. But then word came from Labour MP Gerald Kaufman that the story was 'all over the Commons.'

Macmillan also disregarded the rumours at first. Profumo denied meeting Keeler, and — in retrospect, rather unwisely — Macmillan believed him. He was also untroubled by the possibility that Ivanov was a Russian spy. 'The

Civil Service likes spies they can identify and keep track of,' he tells secretary Timothy Bligh, in the first of several conversations.

At lunch with a girlfriend, Sandra, Ingrams learns about illicit sex in high places. They jokingly try to name the 'Headless Man' photographed in a compromising position with the Duchess of Argyll; and the 'Man in the Mask' who served guests at an orgy attended by several famous and influential people (including Stephen Ward.)

The Profumo affair was first alluded to in a minor magazine, *Westminster Confidential*. But when Keeler failed to appear at Edgecombe's trial, it became clear that trouble was brewing. In one scene, Ingrams talks with a journalist. The reporter refers to a recent front page with the main headline 'MISSING MODEL,' placed alongside a photograph of Profumo 'on the town.'

When another Labour MP, George Wigg, named Keeler as the 'missing witness,' questions were asked in parliament. But Profumo denied it again, and even *The Guardian* accepted his answer, proclaiming 'Mr P Clears the Air.'

Despite his secretary's pleas, Macmillan refused to curtail either *Private Eye* or *That Was the Week That Was*. In another consultation, he explains, 'It's better to be laughed at than ignored.' Though no fan of satire — he was frequently the butt of their jokes — he disliked censorship.

After Keeler's return, another rumour began — that, at Ward's behest, she had asked Profumo to share military secrets. The Home Secretary, Henry Brooke, ordered an investigation into Ward's claim that he had been recruited by MI5 to befriend Ivanov, and — sensationally — that he had helped to mediate in the Cuban Missile Crisis of 1962.

Brooke's search took a sinister turn, however, when Ward was later arrested and spuriously charged with living off immoral earnings. The play conveys the unease Ingrams felt as the scandal he had uncovered turned into a witch-hunt.

Meanwhile, *Private Eye* published 'The Last Days of Macmillan,' a parody of Edward Gibbons' *Decline and Fall of the Roman Empire*. This prompted a visit from an anxious Ward, as the cottage he rented from Lord Astor at Cliveden was denoted by a sign in cod-Latin, reading 'Per Wardua a Astor.' A later scene shows Ward being brushed off by his aristocratic friend.

In another satirical piece, 'Summer Predictions,' the *Private Eye* editors joked that Keeler would soon be appointed Chief Whip. And in a *That Was the Week That Was* skit, a squeaky-voiced impersonator says, 'I'm sure that one day my luck will turn again — especially with all the information that I'm prepared to spill if it doesn't.'

Realising that he could no longer cover up for his friends without implicating himself, Ward calls Timothy Bligh and tells him Profumo lied. He then threatens Macmillan with the prophetic message, 'You have just signed a death warrant for the Conservative government.'

Soon after, Profumo was forced to resign, and Keeler sold her story to the *News of the World*. Macmillan was genuinely shocked to discover Profumo's deception. 'People shouldn't be given what they want just because they want it,' he tells Bligh.

Nonetheless, opposition leader Harold Wilson seized the opportunity to accuse him of 'dereliction of duty.' Nevertheless, the motion was defeated (by a majority of sixty-nine.) But Macmillan was not encouraged: 'They've already decided I'm yesterday's man.'

As Ward's trial reached its grim conclusion, Ingrams deposed Booker as editor-in-chief of *Private Eye*. He then meets Sandra to discuss Ward's suicide. 'How could she sell him out?' Sandra says of Keeler, who had problems of her own.

She then asks Ingrams why the public seems to hate 'good-time girls' like Keeler and Mandy Rice-Davies. 'Because they're young and pretty,' he replies, 'and seem to be having a jolly good time.'

With Ward out of the way, and Lord Denning's report in print, the scandal began to wind down. The Great Train Robbery now dominated the headlines, and as Ingrams observes, the public seemed to have more sympathy with the criminals than their captors.

'Maybe that's Stephen Ward's legacy,' he reflects; 'a deep and abiding scepticism towards the police force.'

In October 1963, Macmillan became seriously ill and swiftly resigned. In a final scene with Bligh, he wishes he could stay, 'if only to disappoint the hordes of satirists.' His secretary tells him that satirists 'are only *Telegraph* readers in waiting' (probably an in-joke, as Booker now writes for the pro-Conservative broadsheet.)

Although Macmillan's fall had long been their aim, the mood at *Private Eye* was not entirely celebratory. Erstwhile impersonator Willie Rushton grouses, 'I've lost my livelihood.' As Harold Wilson wins the 1964 election for Labour, Ingrams says of the new cabinet, 'They're all going to hate us. Isn't it marvellous?'

*This article was originally published at TaraHanks.com on September 26, 2013.*

# SCANDAL '63

*Scandal '63*, currently a wall display in Room 32 of London's National Portrait Gallery, takes its name from journalist Clive Irving's account of the Profumo Affair, published fifty years ago.

The display is divided into small sets, depicting the major figures, the trials and how the scandal influenced art, film and satire. John Profumo, Minister for War in Harold Macmillan's Tory government, is seen at his wedding to actress Valerie Hobson in 1954.

The other photos of Profumo are, in retrospect, ironic. He is shown dancing the Twist with his elegant wife in 1962, boosting his image as a relatively young and glamorous politician. It's easy to imagine why, in contrast to the staid Macmillan, he was once perceived as a possible future Prime Minister. And in a publicity stunt he may have regretted, Profumo visits an army barracks to inspect female officers' uniforms.

His last portrait is a photo-montage, combined with a picture of his erstwhile mistress, Christine Keeler. Though their names have been linked for a half century, they were never photographed together — and, in fact, never crossed paths again after the scandal broke.

Press photos were often telegrammed, accompanied by details of time and place. Among the photographers who covered the Profumo Affair were Kent Gavin (later the *Mirror*'s royal photographer); John Deakin (best-known for documenting London's art scene); and Horace Tonge, whose work has been featured in the *Times* archive. Unnamed others worked for news agencies like Keystone Press, and their photos were syndicated worldwide.

Dr Stephen Ward — the respected osteopath whose fall from grace began when he, perhaps inadvertently, brought the infamous couple together — was also a gifted portraitist. His haunting pastel sketch of Keeler was probably drawn around 1960, when he first encountered her as a dancer at Murray's Cabaret Club in London's West End.

After Ward became the 'fall guy' for the affair, his portraits acquired a certain notoriety, drawing his famous subjects into the headlines. Several were featured on the front page of a British tabloid newspaper, the *Sunday Mirror*, on July 28th — including Lord Astor, at whose Cliveden estate Ward rented a cottage.

Profumo is said to have spotted Keeler (then just 19, and 27 years his junior) while she was taking a late-night swim during a party at Cliveden in the summer of 1961. Another portrait depicts Eugene Ivanov, the Russian naval officer whom Ward met after he was posted to London, at the height of the Cold War. Keeler, who was Ward's flatmate at the time, claims she was briefly involved with Ivanov after meeting Profumo.

That fateful weekend is represented by a group photo, featuring both Ward and Keeler grinning by a swimming pool. They are joined by two of Ward's other protégées — one is Sally Norrie, who would later testify against Ward when he was falsely accused of living off immoral earnings. On June 8th, 1963, the photo was published for the first time.

The blonde on the left was erroneously identified as Mandy Rice-Davies, a friend of Keeler who would later play a role in the scandal. While Davies visited Cliveden as Ward's guest on several occasions, she was absent that weekend — and in fact, she never met Profumo.

But this carefree interlude would soon end. Ward's final days are represented by a series of press photos, showing him arriving at the Old Bailey with journalist Pelham Pound, who was acting as his literary agent; attending the muted reception of an exhibition of his portraits, which coincided with the trial; and leaving court with girlfriend Julie Gulliver on July 24th, 1963 — a week before his fatal overdose.

On June 9th, Keeler testified at the trial of her ex-lover, Lucky Gordon, who was charged with serious assault. She was photographed arriving at court with two other witnesses; her current flatmate, Paula Hamilton-Marshall, and their housekeeper, Olive Brooker. The case was later dismissed on appeal.

Gordon, along with another of Keeler's former boyfriends, Johnny Edgecombe, was photographed on July 10th, arriving by car to testify for Lord Denning, who was compiling an official report. Their journey must have been tense, as the two men had previously brawled over Keeler in a nightclub in October 1962.

In her 1964 memoir, *The Mandy Report* (also known as *My Lives and Lovers*), Mandy Rice-Davies promised to reveal 'the truth, at long last, about the snake-pit masquerading under the title High Society.' Davies was one of the few who attended Ward's exhibition, and two publicity shots from the same period illustrate her unshakable confidence.

In the first, she is the quintessential girl about town, sporting heavy eyeliner and coiffed blonde hair. She smokes a cigarette, and carries a handbag. The second was taken on June 17th, during to a visit to her parents' home in Solihull. Once again, Davies is perfectly groomed in a white polka-dot dress, with her pet poodle on her lap. Perched on a sofa, Davies's sly, knowing expression belies the demure pose; and after all, this young suburbanite was, not long before, the mistress of slum landlord Peter Rachman.

Mandy survived unscathed, whereas Christine found it tougher to live in the spotlight. However, one photograph, taken at the height of the scandal, ensured her a permanent place in our cultural history. It was taken at The Establishment; a Soho club which, for a brief period, hosted some of Britain's finest up-and-coming comedians and musicians.

The shoot was in black and white. Artfully naked, Keeler sat on a backward-facing chair. Her face is in profile, and her expression is enigmatic: defiant, yet fragile. Her photographer, Lewis Morley, was Australian; and like Keeler, he was always somewhat puzzled by the success of his image. It became a symbol of the 1960s, but for both artist and model it was something of a mixed blessing. It was first published in the *Sunday Mirror* on June 9th.

Morley died on September 13 this year, leaving his photos and correspondence with Keeler, along with his other famous works from the era, to the National Media Museum in Bradford.

The photo session was arranged to publicise a film based on the scandal, which Keeler was to star in. It was eventually shot with actress Yvonne Buckingham. Keeler provided a short introduction, which was badly dubbed. She was photographed by Tom Blau in what was described as a 'screen test.' She had been smuggled into the studio for filming.

That November, Keeler was profiled in US film magazine, *Modern Screen* — featuring Blau's stills and another from the Morley session. 'Chris has always wanted to be a star,' the article read, adding that she 'expects to make a mint from this movie.' However, the film was never released in Britain, and remains obscure. It has been variously titled *The Keeler Affair* and *The Christine Keeler Story*.

Founded in 1961, *Private Eye* came into its own as the Profumo Affair unfolded. Its June 14, 1963 issue featured Harold Macmillan, in a parody of Keeler's nude portrait by cartoonist Gerald Scarfe. The caption reads, 'Only one man was in a position to cover up for his friends.' A caricature of Keeler herself — by another artist, Barry Fantoni — adorns the cover of *That Affair*, a satirical LP. Among the tracks are titles like 'Dimbleby at Cliveden,' and 'The Little White Lie That Jack Told.'

In the autumn of 1963, pop artist Pauline Boty began work on a painting, also called 'Scandal '63.' An early version of the painting shows Keeler leaving her flat, after a press photo. However, she later replaced this image with the now more famous Morley pose. Profumo and the other men are reduced to a row of headshots above Keeler's full body. Unfortunately, the painting was lost after Boty's tragic death in 1966, and only a few photos exist of the work-in-progress.

My sole criticism of *Scandal '63* is that it is rather a small display, and that a catalogue has not been published. *Christine Keeler: My Life in Pictures*, a 2010 exhibition at London's Mayor Gallery, was accompanied by a book including modelling photographs from the 1960s, and pop art by Jean-Jacques Lebel, one of the first to recognise Keeler's iconic potential.

In recent years, the British artist Stella Vine — who, like Christine, was once a dancer in a Soho strip club — has painted her several times, using tabloid photos to depict key moments in the scandal. Speaking to *The Observer* in 2006, shortly after the death of John Profumo — and his subsequent deification in the press — Vine said she was drawn to Keeler's image, as depicted by Lewis Morley. 'In that photograph you just have that spirit of something, an incredible sexual thing: something in the eyes that takes you way beyond it being a Page Three of someone just wanting a couple of hundred quid for a photo.'

'It is almost like Christine Keeler has herself become a prism,' Bo Gorzelak Pedersen commented recently, while reviewing a series of oil paintings by London-based artist Fionn Wilson. 'In one portrait we see one side of Keeler, in another we see a different side — and when seen together, they strangely mirror each other. What appears is a faceted image of a real woman, not a cultural icon, or just a victim, or just a sex symbol, but a person. Which is what love does, it lets the person come forth.'

*This article was first published at TaraHanks.com on September 9, 2013.*

# IT'S A SCANDAL! SONGS FOR SOHO BLONDES

It was 'the era of *Peeping Tom* and the Profumo Affair,' in 'the London of Colin Wilson and Christine Keeler,' writes Bob Stanley (of Saint Etienne fame) in the sleeve notes to *It's a Scandal! Songs for Soho Blondes*, a 2013 compilation from the Fantastic Voyage label. The cover is in the style of a red-top front page, with an insouciant Mandy Rice-Davies surrounded by faceless men, toasting her with champagne.

'Soho in the fifties had a village existence by day,' Stanley notes, adding that 'the queue of men outside the Windmill Theatre suggested it became quite different at night.' Mandy Rice-Davies, a sixteen year-old from Birmingham first met Christine Keeler (two years her senior) when she joined the chorus line at Murray's Cabaret Club on Beak Street.

'The music on *It's a Scandal*,' he reflects, 'feels particularly English.' This type of Englishness is defined as 'sauce with a hint of whiplash.' Here was a hidden world where 'the man in the raincoat to your left could be a vicar, a Russian spy, or even the Chancellor of the Exchequer.'

By the 1970s, Soho was 'grubbier and more furtive.' In the 1990s, the area was 'cleaned up' as part of an ongoing process of gentrification, making it unaffordable to the showgirls and bohemians who once called it home. Beyond Soho, however, burlesque has made a comeback — perhaps in response to the ubiquity of porn, giving the pin-up era an aura of nostalgic elegance.

'Miss X' was the pseudonym of a witness in the trial of Stephen Ward for living off immoral earnings, and was adopted by Joyce Blair for her single, 'Christine,' which capitalised on the scandal. It made the charts in August 1963 — the same month Ward died after taking a fatal overdose. Blair revealed her true identity during an interview for the first episode of ITV's cult music programme, *Ready Steady Go!*

Over a Latin jazz instrumental, Miss X introduces herself: 'My name is Christine, what's yours?' With faux innocence, she protests, 'But I'm a good girl!' She scolds her imaginary lover, and all listeners — 'I *told* you I was good.' We hear laughter, slaps, moans. And at last, the final irony: 'Your secret is safe with me.'

While Keeler's provocative image inspired artists, photographers and musicians, Mandy Rice-Davies became a minor entertainer in her own right. 'Close Your Eyes,' from the *Introducing Mandy* EP (1964), begins with a saxophone solo, while Mandy's 'double-tracked and breathy' vocals are encased within an orchestral backdrop. 'Let's pretend that we're both young and chic,' she purrs to a sugar daddy.

Born at Tiger Bay, Cardiff in 1937, Shirley Bassey emerged in the late 1950s as one of the greatest black British singers of her generation. Her 1957 EP, *Shirley Bassey at the Café de Paris*, included the rather risqué 'Sex.' Like Mandy, she appears wise beyond her years. 'From morn to night I hear the woes/Of the mixed-up Janes and mixed-up Joes,' she regales the audience in a wry spoken prelude.

'Freud has a word for it,' the song begins. The lyrics owe something to Cole Porter's 'Let's Do It,' as Shirley drops some of the era's most famous names: 'Fortunes are spent on it/Monroe pays the rent on it.'

'It,' of course, is sex – this was the age of the Kinsey Report. Post-war repression still reigned supreme, but trouble was brewing. 'Most husbands are blamed for it,' Shirley sings. 'The man always pays for it...'

Lucille Mapp – who would leave fame behind in 1963 – recorded a gold-digger's anthem, 'Chinchilla,' in 1959. Extolling the joys of wearing fur is just one of many activities celebrated in this collection that would be frowned upon today. 'Diamonds Are a Girl's Best Friend,' immortalised by Marilyn Monroe in the 1953 film, *Gentlemen Prefer Blondes*, is rebuffed in the lyrics: 'Diamonds are a friendship ring/Chinchilla makes the love-bells ring.' But the Trinidadian Ms Mapp's feline delivery owes more to Eartha Kitt.

'Your eyes are lighted windows/There's a party going on inside.' Actress Diana Dors – Britain's answer to Monroe – brought a hint of danger to 'Rollercoaster Blues,' taken from her classic 1960 album, *Swingin' Dors* (now a collector's item.) Diana was grittier than Marilyn, and could pull off vulgarity in style.

There's nothing wholesome about this lover: 'You're slick and evil,' Diana croons, 'Just like your patent leather shoes.' A certain masochism is implied when she confesses, 'You spoiled me baby/And now the carousel's too tame for me.'

The blonde star's publicity-seeking antics and wild lifestyle often overshadowed her innate talent. Following her separation from a controlling first husband Dennis Hamilton in 1958, a cash-strapped Dors shocked Britain by telling newspapers about the sex parties held at their London home.

Christine Keeler, who subsequently occupied the property with Stephen Ward, recalled finding a two-way mirror there. 'It had pride of place up on the sitting-room wall,' she wrote. 'It wasn't until later that I found out the mirror had a crack in it — Diana, apparently, had broken it and it didn't work anymore.'

Many of the tracks on this compilation are movie tie-ins. 'Make Mine Mink,' recorded by the Knightsbridge Chorale, accompanied an eponymous heist comedy, starring Terry Thomas. Elke Sommer, a Berlin-born actress — and daughter of a Lutheran minister — contributed 'Be Not Notty' to *Why Bother to Knock*, a 1961 farce (not to be confused with the 1952 film noir, *Don't Bother to Knock*.) On this novelty record, Sommer's vocal, mostly spoken, is a verbal tease: 'That's enough of love and passion/Don't you think you've had your ration?'

Moving away from blondes, sultry Anne Heywood (born Violet Pretty in Birmingham) recorded 'Love Is' for *The Heart of a Man* (1959), in which she starred alongside heartthrob singer Frankie Vaughan. 'Love is a red-hot candle/Love is a white-hot scandal,' she riffs moodily, to a jazzy, syncopated tune.

Maxine Daniels, a Londoner of Caribbean heritage, was a popular jazz singer who worked with bandleader Humphrey Lyttleton, among others. 'Lola's Heart,' a calypso ditty about an island girl who bewitches passing sailors, was included in the soundtrack of *Passionate Summer* (1958.)

The Barry Sisters, an American duo whose career dated back to the 1940s, covered a jazz standard, 'Why Don't You Do Right,' in 1960. Whereas Peggy Lee's more famous rendition is half-mournful, the Barry Sisters had a sassier style.

The Eric Winstone Orchestra's piano-led 'Piccadilly Third Stop' was theme to a 1960 thriller of the same title. *The Shakedown*, another crime thriller released that year, features a bluesy number performed by Sheila Buxton in a nightclub scene. Lynn Cornell — best-known for her theme to *Never on Sunday*, starring Melina Mercouri — released another, more obscure single in 1960. 'Demon Lover' exudes sexual threat: 'I never knew there was such love for anyone to give/Until my demon lover's back I don't want to live.'

Now almost forgotten, Jeri Southern was a contemporary of Julie London and other post-war American singers. Frank Sinatra called her 'the very best.' In 'Run,' one of Southern's final releases before retirement in 1959, her soft voice creates a sense of intimacy. 'Run as fast as you can run,' she warns. 'From those who say our love is done/Because it's none of their affair.' In a morally rigid society, love — or pre-marital sex — was always a provocation. 'Run from every rumour they've begun,' she urges her paramour.

The exotic was also erotic, as the Beverley Sisters discovered in 'The Sphinx Won't Tell' (1961.) 'The wide Sahara we will roam/I've decided to leave my veil at home,' they trill. As Bob Stanley remarks, the wholesome trio 'never sounded saucier.' Commencing with a gong, Geoff Love's orchestration employs every Egyptian cliché. It's easy to imagine Christine and Mandy dancing to this at Murray's, dressed as slave-girls with heavy eyeliner.

A fixture on television, Valerie Masters released 'Say When' as a B-side in 1959. 'So when you're ready to give in/All you gotta do is say when,' she pipes breezily. She would later work with the fabled English producer, Joe Meek.

Instrumentals like 'The Jazz Scene' (by The Jazz Stars, 1962) provided a soundtrack to the coffee bars where teenagers thronged, copping beatnik poses. Beryl Bryden — once described by Ella Fitzgerald as 'Britain's Queen of the Blues' — was one of the few English jazz singers not to fake an American accent. 'Moanin',' a B-side from 1962, was inspired by Art Blakey's 1958 instrumental. Bob Stanley describes it as 'a musical equivalent to the opening sequence of Powell and Pressburger's *Peeping Tom*.'

New Yorker Linda Laurie, a singer-songwriter, had a minor hit with the oddball 'Ambrose (Part 5)' in 1959. On the flipside, 'Ooh What a Lover,' she repeats the title phrase while a male chorus replies, 'You've got so many other lovers/You make me feel so tragic ...'

In 1962, Yorkshire's Marion Ryan — dubbed 'the Marilyn Monroe of popular song' — covered 'An Occasional Man,' previously recorded by Sarah Vaughan and others. 'My little island is such a beauty/You may forget to hear the call of duty,' she quips.

Swedish actress Anita Lindblom's 1962 B-side, 'Mr Big Wheel,' is the opposite of a gold-digger's anthem. To a brassy, big band sound, she mocks an ex-lover who is living the high-life: 'A fool with money must have his fling/Roll on Mr Big Wheel, roll ... '

'Send Me,' from the 1961 revue, *One Over the Eight*, was an early composition by Lionel Bart. Singer Toni Eden also values love over money: 'I've had just about everything you can name/Except for the fire within me that's gonna take two to set aflame.' In 'Love Me Now! Love Me Now! Love Me Now!', Sylvia Sands — a regular guest on the BBC's *Drumbeat* in 1959 — is equally assertive: 'Take me while I'm younger and bolder/Take me before I'm older and colder ... '

Eve Boswell, who found fame in South Africa, made her name in Britain during the 1950s. 'Wimoweh Cha Cha,' from the EP *Eve at Ciro*'s, is a sinuous take on 'The Lion Sleeps Tonight,' recorded live in Johannesburg.

*It's a Scandal!* closes with the flipside of its opening track. In a cabaret turn, Miss X muses, 'What a shame that every name men give to it/Can't conceal its fame or save their shameless necks/They say it's the jewel in life's crown, but boiling it down/It's simply S-E-X.'

It's hard not to see this as a direct commentary on Profumo, Ward and the other men caught up in the turmoil of 1963. Within a year, The Beatles would revive English music and 'the Sixties' would truly begin. But although the songs on *It's a Scandal* are pre-Sexual Revolution, they are far from timid.

From coy innuendo to outright burlesque, the Soho blondes often seem bolder than the 'dollybirds' who replaced them.

# ABOUT THE AUTHOR

Tara Hanks was born and raised in London. Since then she has lived in Lancaster, Derby and now Brighton. She is married and has two sons. The author of two novels, *Wicked Baby* (2004) and *The Mmm Girl* (2008), she is also co-author (with Eric Woodard) of *Jeanne Eagels: A Life Revealed* (2015.) Tara writes about aspects of popular culture for various websites and magazines, and maintains the *ES Updates* blog. She is currently working on her third novel.

www.tarahanks.com

Printed in Great Britain
by Amazon